Secrets...
& Ambition

...Plus!

ARE YOU A DRAMA QUEEN?
TRY OUR FAB QUIZ AT
THE BACK OF THE BOOK

SOME SECRETS ARE JUST TOO GOOD TO KEEP TO YOURSELF!

Sugar
SECRETS...

...& Ambition

Mel Sparke

Collins
An Imprint of HarperCollins*Publishers*

Published in Great Britain by Collins in 1999
Collins is an imprint of HarperCollins*Publishers* Ltd
77–85 Fulham Palace Road, Hammersmith, London W6 8JB

The HarperCollins website address is
www.**fire**and**water**.com

9 8 7 6 5 4 3 2 1

Creative consultant: Karen McCombie
Copyright © Sugar 1999. Licensed with TLC

ISBN 0 00 675438 4

Printed and bound in Great Britain by
Caledonian International Book Manufacturing Ltd, Glasgow

CHAPTER 1

• •

THE GATECRASHER

"There's something odd about him."

"Mmm. He looks shifty."

"He looks *really* shifty."

"Yeah, like a criminal or something."

"What's he up to?"

Sonja Harvey turned questioningly to her cousin Catrina Osgood. Catrina stopped chewing for a second as she stared thoughtfully at the fidgety boy on the other side of the room. Slowly, she blew out a huge, rubbery pink blob of bubblegum – the exact shade of her mini dress – and let it pop before she finally responded.

"*I* know what's wrong with him," she nodded to herself and a knowing smile crept across her face. "He's panicking."

Sonja wrinkled her nose and peered through

the huddle of chatting party-goers at the dark-haired lad. She wasn't convinced by Cat's theory. What did Matt have to panic about?

He was hosting yet another of his brilliant parties. He had one arm around his girlfriend, Gabrielle, who looked as though she was having a great time. And her friends – who'd come along to the party too – seemed to be practically as mad on Matt as Gabrielle was. They'd been twittering around him all evening so far, like he was some chart-topping superstar and they were his adoring fans.

Perfect for Matt, really, Sonja mused. *Surrounded by a posse of pretty young things. It's his dream come true!*

"But why would he be panicking?" she asked Cat, raising her voice above the music.

"Look around this place," said Cat, with a sweeping gesture at the dozens of people cluttering up Matt Ryan's huge basement den. "See – there's Sarah Thomson... Emma Brant... Alison wotsit... that redhead who's a friend of the guy from Central Sounds... Karen Lunn... that girl with the big nose who was in the year above you... Josie Wilson, Susie Cunningham's sister... oh, *and* Susie Cunningham. They're all here. And at one time or another, Matt's snogged the lot of them."

"Including you," added Sonja.

"Including me," Cat nodded, unperturbed at the thought of being just one more notch on her friend Matt's long list of conquests. After all, there were enough boys here tonight that she had dated. "And, of course, our Matt is terrified that one of them is going to blow his cover."

"As long as it's not you," warned Sonja, then turned her gaze back to Matt.

A fake smile was plastered across his face and his eyes constantly raked the room like a minesweeper, on the look out for unexploded bombs in the shape of tactless exes.

"It's amazing, really, that he's been able to keep Gabrielle in the dark about his past for this long."

"Yeah, but it's a load of rubbish, isn't it?" Cat sneered. "It's not like he's a bank robber or axe murderer or something. What's he trying to hide from her? He's only snogged some girls."

"Well, a whole *load* of girls," smirked Sonja.

Cat grinned widely. "OK, so maybe it *would* be easier to count the girls he *hasn't* snogged in Winstead."

"Who are you two being horrible about?" asked Maya Joshi, wandering back to her friends after getting caught up in a million conversations on her way to the loo and back.

"Matt," answered Sonja and Cat in unison.

"Uh-huh," nodded Maya, glancing over at the object of their ridicule. "I see he's still in a panic about being found out then."

"*See?*" Cat nudged Sonja, happy to have her diagnosis confirmed, even though Sonja hadn't been contradicting her.

"He should have been honest with Gabrielle in the first place," continued Maya. "Just because *she* hasn't been out with anyone before, it doesn't mean she expects *him* to be Mr Squeaky Clean."

"Yeah, but he's just been a big wimp about all of this, hasn't he?" shrugged Cat, idly twirling a pink string of bubblegum around her finger.

Sonja and Maya sniggered at the idea of Matt being described as a wimp. Handsome, hunky, drop-dead gorgeous... that was the way most girls thought of him. But not his girl mates. Not Cat (well, not any more); not Sonja (although she'd tried to); and certainly not Maya or Kerry, or even Anna.

They all knew that behind that good-looking exterior was a sometimes insecure, tactless boy, with zero common sense, a tendency to be a bit selfish, but who was also sweet and funny when he wanted to be. And right now, he was definitely being a wimp.

"It's like, the longer he's avoided telling her, the worse it gets," Cat went on. "Tonight, for instance, he can't even enjoy his own party for worrying. How's it going to sound when Gabrielle finally finds out that she's the last in a long line of females who've had intimate knowledge of her boyfriend's tonsils?"

"Like I said before," Sonja leaned closer to her cousin, her eyes wide and serious, "just don't let it be *you* who lets slip. We all promised Matt that we wouldn't tell..."

"Even if we all do think it's a really stupid idea," Maya chipped in.

"...and you, Madam," Sonja continued, pointing a finger at Cat, "have come far too close to opening your big gob at times."

"Me?" squeaked Cat, all innocence. "I'd *never*—"

"Yes, you would, so don't waste your breath," Maya chided her good-naturedly. "Like Sonja says, it's up to Matt to tell Gabrielle."

"Unless he has a heart attack first..." Cat muttered sulkily.

● ● ●

Over the other side of the room, Matt wiped a few trickling beads of sweat from his forehead, unaware of Cat's typically catty comment. He was feeling stressed all right.

When he'd first started going out with Gabrielle, he'd been so stunned when she'd admitted that he was her first ever boyfriend that he'd done something really stupid. He'd told her he'd only ever had two girlfriends (which was just about as far from the truth as it was possible to get).

He'd also omitted the fact that he and Cat had dated, and continually dreaded that his mischievous mate would spill the beans to Gabrielle (she'd been close to it plenty of times). He wished now that he'd told Gabrielle straight out; it would have been better, he knew. But the longer he left it, the bigger a deal it became. So Matt took the coward's way out and said nothing.

Having this party was a bad idea, he decided. Too late. There were just way too many opportunities for hints to be dropped and gaffes to be made.

Already, when he'd gone up to the loo, Danny Eccleston's sister had pinched his bum and flirtily told him off for never phoning her after their date. The trouble was, Matt could only vaguely remember the date, months before, and certainly couldn't remember the girl's name. What if Gabrielle had been around to witness that? What if... wots-'er-name tried it on again later, in full view of Gabrielle or any of her mates?

"Matt?" a voice interrupted his fretting. "Who are those three girls over there? They're staring."

Matt gazed down blankly at the questioning face of Gabrielle's best mate and then looked in the direction she was pointing.

"Oh, them!" he said with a huge amount of relief. He'd half expected to see a huddle of mutinous and irate exes standing on the far side of the room, plotting his downfall, but instead it was just the girls.

He gave a wobbly, relieved smile and wiggled his fingers limply at Maya, Sonja and Cat. In return he got a wry smile (Maya), a thumbs-up (Sonja) and a tongue stuck out (Cat).

"They're cool," he said to Gabrielle's friend. "They're my mates."

"Oh," shrugged Angelique, pacified. "I just wondered."

Matt nodded and didn't know what else to say. Nerves had emptied his mind of any of his usual silver-tongued charm – or even straightforward banter. The other problem was, he was finding it hard to put names to the faces of Gabrielle's five friends; apart from her best mate Angelique, whom he'd met in passing, he'd never set eyes on the other four till tonight.

And what a waste, he thought ruefully, aware that he was the envy of most of the lads in the room. *I'm so wound up that I can't even enjoy the fact that I'm surrounded by six very cute girls.*

When Matt had first discovered that Gabrielle was only fourteen, he hadn't been sure what to do. At eighteen, and being someone who considered himself super-cool, he momentarily wasn't sure if going out with someone so much younger was quite the right image. But knowing Gabrielle's age didn't change the fact that she was gorgeous, fun-loving, had loads in common with him – and simply made him *glow*, all the way through. The fact that she'd fitted into the crowd so easily confirmed things, and Matt had been able to relax.

But not tonight. Tonight he felt that his past had come back to torment him with a vengeance. He was acutely aware of not just the difference in their ages, but in their experience.

A squeeze around Matt's waist made him look round into Gabrielle's smiling face.

"Hey," she whispered in his ear, standing on tiptoe to do it, "Jasmine says she quite fancies Joe!"

Matt scanned the faces of the four girls grinning at him and wondered which one was Jasmine. And which one was Gemma and which one was Lauren. And which one was Caitlin, for that matter...

"Do you think Joe might be interested?" asked Gabrielle, raising her dark eyebrows.

Matt might not have known which was which when it came to the girls, but they all seemed friendly and nice, as well as pretty. Though what shy-boy Joe Gladwin would make of having an admirer was anyone's guess.

The last time that had happened – when Joe and Matt had met two girls at a birthday party where Matt was DJing – it hadn't ended well. The girl who'd come on to Joe frightened him half to death *and* she'd ended up slapping him for ignoring her.

Scanning the room, Matt noticed that Joe was over by the sound system, talking animatedly with two males. Peering closer, he recognised them as Billy and Andy who played in The Loud with Joe and Ollie.

He has to be talking music, Matt decided. *Nothing else gets Joe going like that.*

"Should we get him to come over?" suggested Gabrielle.

Matt's mind raced – he didn't know how to handle this. Joe would run a mile if he got a whiff of the fact that he was being set up, and Matt hadn't a clue how to do it subtly.

He needed to ask Ollie for advice, but where on earth was Ollie? He and Kerry hadn't shown up yet and that wasn't like them; they hadn't said anything about not being able to come tonight.

"I, uh..." Matt faffed, not wanting to deny Gabrielle anything, including pairing her mate off with his.

But before he could waffle any more, Matt felt a tidal wave of panic engulf him as he spotted Ollie and Kerry finally making an appearance at the door of the den – with a very unexpected and not entirely welcome guest...

CHAPTER 2

● ●

ATMOSPHERICS

Anna Michaels had read an interesting article in a magazine about intuition. The gist of it was that everyone should try to develop their instincts more: try to feel what others are feeling, aim to sense moods and changes.

She'd been giving it a whirl in the café all week and was quite pleased with the results. When a grumpy young mum had come in with her baby on Wednesday afternoon, Anna had sensed that her snappiness while ordering was due to tiredness, not nastiness.

"What a beautiful baby," Anna had complimented the woman as she placed a cup of tea in front of her. "Is he always such a little angel?" "Not during the night, when he wakes up wailing *every* hour *on* the hour." The woman had given her an ironic smile. "Still," Anna had continued, trying to lighten the young mum's mood, "I bet he makes up for it by being adorable the rest of the time." "Yes, yes, he does," the woman had positively beamed.

By sensing the mood and then saying the right thing, Anna was sure she'd made a difference. But she hadn't got it right all the time.

When Dorothy had arrived for her shift on Thursday, Anna sensed that something wasn't right and worried that the pensioner was feeling ill. "Everything all right, Dorothy?" she'd asked. "No," grumbled the grey-haired woman as she pulled on her apron. "My stupid daughter-in-law phoned me last night – *right* at the beginning of *Coronation Street*! Missed the whole thing!"

Anna put her miscalculation down to inexperience, but still felt that there was something in it. She might yet have a talent for this intuition business.

Like tonight. As she walked back down the stairs into the basement room with a big bag of Kettle crisps she'd got from the kitchen, Anna could feel a chill spread over her. One quick glance round didn't throw up any obvious clues – the room was still heaving with music and talk and people, and the occasional dancer. So what was it?

Anna took the last step into the den and slid her back along the wall to the left of the entrance. She tried to concentrate, taking a deep breath and a longer, slower look around.

Over to her right, Sonja and Cat were still perched where she'd last seen them on a long, low set of drawers, with Maya standing alongside. They were all transfixed by something in the middle of the room, but Anna couldn't make out who or what it was because of the crowd of shouty boys directly in front of her.

She felt her eyes being drawn suddenly to the opposite wall where Matt was still standing, surrounded by Gabrielle's mates. Even in the darkened room his face looked shockingly white, as if all the blood had been drained from it, while the girls partied on unwittingly.

"Anna!" said a voice in her ear.

She turned to find Joe at her side, with Billy and Andy hovering behind by Matt's towering racks of CDs.

"Hey, Joe!" she smiled, then realised he too looked uncomfortable and very glad to see her. She must have only been out of the room for about twenty minutes – she'd got chatting while she was raiding the kitchen – but something dramatic had happened in that short space of time, that was for sure.

"You'll never guess who's shown up," Joe half grinned, half winced.

"Who?"

"Ollie's twin sister, Natasha," said Joe, rolling his eyes to indicate trouble.

Only Anna couldn't figure out quite what the trouble was. She knew Matt and Natasha had gone out together briefly, which would be uncomfortable for Matt right now, but it didn't totally explain the wave of tension she could sense.

And it also didn't explain why Cat and Sonja in particular looked less than ecstatic.

Joe spotted her perplexed expression and realised that Anna, who was still relatively new to the crowd, wouldn't realise the full implication of what he was saying.

"Natasha isn't exactly popular with anyone – well, except Ollie, of course," Joe explained. "Like with Cat – you know that she used to go out with Matt?"

Anna nodded and gazed over at Cat, who seemed to be smouldering with animosity. Yes, Anna knew about their past relationship; she'd been there when Matt had made them all promise not to tell Gabrielle about his ridiculously long list of ex-girlfriends, which included Cat.

But why would Cat's fur stand on end with

this particular girl? wondered Anna. *Isn't this whole party full of his cast-offs?*

"Y'see," began Joe, about to shed light on the whole affair, "Natasha is the reason they split – Matt snogged her in front of... well, all of us."

Loads of pieces of the puzzle slotted together for Anna; snatches of conversation that hadn't meant anything to her before she'd got to know Ollie and his friends properly now made sense.

"Tasha's been out with us occasionally since then and Cat's tried to be civil to her for Ollie's sake," Joe continued, "but she really can't stand her. It's just a bit humiliating for her, y'know?"

Anna's gaze now flipped from Catrina to the visibly quaking Matt. Joe followed her gaze.

"Matt's problem is—"

"He doesn't want Natasha blurting out anything in front of Gabrielle," Anna interrupted, sure of that connection at least.

"Oh, no – it's not just that," Joe shook his head. "It's also the fact that Natasha thinks Matt's the biggest, sleaziest scumbag around."

"Why? He's a bit, well... y'know. But he's not sleazy!"

Anna didn't have to explain that to Joe. Like all the friends, they knew Matt was a bit too sure of his own attractiveness, but he didn't deserve – Anna felt sure – to be labelled *that* badly.

"It's a long story," shrugged Joe, "but, basically, *ages* ago, Natasha picked up something he said all wrong and thought he was a total lech. Matt was really hurt, and Ollie's tried to straighten it out heaps of times, but Natasha's never listened. Matt's tried his best to be all friendly with her since, but that's never worked either."

"So, is she here with Ollie and Kerry tonight?" asked Anna, peering through the crush of bodies in front of her, but still not managing to catch sight of the object of their conversation.

"Yeah, and that's the *other* problem..."

"What is?" asked Anna, trying hard to keep up.

"Natasha's a bit of a sore subject between Kerry and Sonja. There was a time when Sonja got really into being Tasha's best mate – y'know? Got stars in her eyes about hanging out with this glamorous model from London," explained Joe. "There was a lot of bad feeling because Kerry felt elbowed out."

Anna nodded. She could see how Kerry, who didn't have copious amounts of self-esteem, might struggle with that situation.

"And then apart from all that," continued Joe, "Sonja got pretty miffed when Natasha dropped her like a brick when she went back to work."

"So," Anna grinned ruefully, "what's she done to upset Maya?"

"Oh, nothing," Joe grinned back. "Maya's too smart to let Natasha bother her."

"And you?"

Joe shrugged awkwardly, shoving his hands deep in his pockets. "I might have been her brother's best mate for years, but I don't think I'm the kind of lad that girls like Natasha even know exist."

But Anna was only half listening to Joe's self-deprecating remark.

"Look," she nudged him, her eyes glued to the right-hand side of the cavernous room.

"Uh-oh..." breathed Joe.

● ● ●

"She's coming over! Can you believe the cheek of her?" Cat hissed to Sonja and Maya.

"Try and be nice, Cat," Maya hissed back, "for Ollie's sake. Go on – you've done it before."

Natasha slunk towards them as if she was on a catwalk, watched closely by the crowd of lads that had been blocking Anna's view earlier. On the far side of the room, Sonja could see Kerry heaving her shoulders up helplessly in her friends' direction. Matt had stepped away from Gabrielle and her friends, and appeared to be having a frantic conversation with Ollie, from what Sonja could make out.

Was Ollie trying to explain what he was doing bringing his sister – not exactly Matt's biggest fan – along tonight? Sonja wondered.

"Sonja!" smiled Natasha, greeting her like a long-lost buddy.

Stunned into silence, Sonja gawped at the perfectly made-up face, the blunt-cut, silky hair and the open, guiltless expression.

Doesn't she remember that she just dumped on me? thought Sonja, thinking back with hurt pride how she'd once gone out of her way to befriend Natasha and hadn't had so much as a postcard or a hello via Ollie for her trouble.

"You look great!" Natasha gushed, kissing a startled Sonja on both cheeks in a very luvvie way.

Wait a minute, Sonja realised in a flash. *She doesn't get it – she has no idea that I was upset!*

For a second, Sonja wanted to be angry with Natasha; to get her to see how tactless and thoughtless she'd been. But what was the point? Presumably in Natasha's hectic, high-flying life, she didn't have time to take friendships as seriously as Sonja did. The fact that Natasha was so busy didn't make it right, but, Sonja reconciled herself, it did make her a little sad.

"Hi, Tasha," she managed to smile, pleased in spite of herself that the most attractive, special person in the room had made a beeline straight for her.

Cat managed to bare her teeth in a sarcastically cheesy grin in response to Natasha's half-hearted "Hello" in her direction (Tasha wasn't any fonder of Cat than Cat was of her).

"How are you, Tasha?" asked Maya, her good manners distracting Natasha from Cat's lack of them. She hoped.

"Fine thanks, Maya," Natasha nodded. "Been busy. Doing the shows, y'know."

"Oh, dahling – what a drag, schweetie," Cat muttered sarcastically under her breath. Natasha didn't seem to hear, although Maya and Sonja most certainly did.

"It's good to see you," Natasha smiled, turning her attention back to Sonja.

"Yeah?" Sonja was flattered, though she couldn't relax. Not when she could see Catrina pulling faces out of the corner of her eye.

"I was hoping you'd be here," Natasha smiled at her.

"I doubt that Matt was hoping *you'd* be here," Cat interrupted suddenly.

"*Sorry*?" snapped Natasha, her eyes flashing a glare of disdain at Catrina and her pink Barbie doll get-up.

"It's a long story," Maya tried to diffuse the

situation. "What she means is that Matt's got a new girlfriend and he—"

"He doesn't want his exes hanging around, ruining his night!" came Cat's hissed interruption.

"*Me?*" gasped Natasha, wide-eyed. "What about you! You went out with him too!"

"Well, yes I did – until Miss 'I'm a model' Stanton decided to nick him off me!"

"I decided to nick him off you? I don't think so!" Natasha barked back. "That creep was two-timing you, more like. As far as I'm concerned, you two losers were perfect for each other! And the only reason I'm at sleazoid Matt Ryan's party is that Ollie begged me to come."

"Cat, come and help me get everyone some more drinks," suggested Maya, skilfully scooping her startled friend off the chest of drawers and dragging her away before she could protest.

Sonja, reeling from the speed at which the Natasha/Cat collision had happened and marvelling at Maya's diplomatic manoeuvrings, only now spotted who was standing directly behind Natasha – Kerry, Ollie, an ashen-faced Matt and a slightly startled-looking Gabrielle.

Where did they spring from? worried Sonja. *And just how much of that did Gabrielle catch?*

CHAPTER 3

• •

ALL IN THE BEST POSSIBLE TASTE

"I'm 99 per cent sure that she didn't hear anything."

"Really?" asked Ollie dubiously as he brushed past Matt carrying a full tray of Sunday morning breakfasts. The End-of-the-Line café where he worked was a favourite recovery joint for people who'd overdone it on Saturday nights.

"Yeah," nodded Matt, getting up from his counterside stool and traipsing after his friend. "She just caught the tail-end of Cat and Natasha sniping at each other, but she didn't suss out why."

"Well," sighed Ollie, plonking dishes in front of punters and pushing past Matt as he headed back towards the kitchen, "I did warn Natasha to keep schtum in front of Gabrielle. About you and her and everything."

"But I bet she'd have *loved* to blab, knowing what she thinks of me. Why is it girls can be so bitchy?" grumbled Matt, trailing after Ollie and flopping back down on his stool while Ollie disappeared into the kitchen to pick up more orders for the crowded café.

"Listen," said Ollie, emerging, laden, through the kitchen doorway again, "don't bad-mouth my sister *too* much, Matt. I know you're my mate, but she is my sister and you didn't exactly play fair by her when you snogged her back at our birthday party. Remember – *you* knew you were going out with Cat; she didn't!"

Matt rose up from his perch and followed Ollie puppy dog-style across the crowded café again.

"No, no, mate – I understand! But you have to realise, I don't want anyone to mess up what I have with Gabrielle..."

Ollie, who was busy trying to keep all of the customers happy, was fast losing patience with Matt. He didn't have time for Matt's self-pity right now.

"Matt," shrugged Ollie, clutching his now empty tray to his chest, "the only one likely to mess things up with Gabrielle is you, if you don't play straight with her."

"But, Ol!" Matt protested, tagging behind him again. "Last night—"

"Look, Natasha turned up out of the blue yesterday afternoon and seemed pretty down. Mum and Dad were working in the pub, so what was I supposed to do? Just leave her sitting at home all night?" Ollie practically barked. "I thought bringing her to your party would be fine; if I told her to be cool about it, *you'd* be cool about it. Sorry if I got that wrong!"

"No, of course not!" Matt tried to pacify him, aware that he'd annoyed Ollie somehow, but unsure how it had swung around from himself being put out to Ollie suddenly getting uptight. "It's OK; I know she's your sister and all, and I know I should have come clean with Gaby—"

"Matt, why don't you go and sit down and tell Sonja all of this?" Ollie cut him off impatiently, his pencil poised as he tried to take yet another order.

Matt looked over dubiously at Sonja, who was sitting at the booth by the window, skimming through a Sunday supplement magazine that had been left behind by a previous customer.

"Nah, I'll just wait at the counter till you're a bit quieter," he swallowed nervously.

Ollie sighed and turned his attention back to his tableful of customers. He knew why Matt didn't fancy sitting alone with Sonja. He'd heard her tell Matt sternly that she wanted to have a word with him as soon as she'd walked in.

("We've all had enough of this keeping secrets stuff – it's got to stop!") Sonja was obviously gearing up to giving him a lecture – and Matt was clearly not in the mood to hear it.

Scribbling furiously on his little pad, Ollie didn't pay any attention to the bell tinkling as the café door was pushed open, but he certainly took notice when a cool pair of hands slithered across his eyes.

"Guess who?" said an instantly recognisable voice.

"Tasha," sighed Ollie, wrestling her hands from his face and gazing apologetically at the couple he'd been trying to serve. "Can't you see I'm working?"

"Ooh, spoilsport!" his sister sulked, pulling a face but still managing to look pretty. "I come to see my darling brother and all I get is a mouthful of abuse…"

"You mean you got bored hanging out at home so you thought you'd come down and pester me," he smiled, his eyes back on the pad as he finished writing the last of the order.

With a final flourish of his pencil, he looked up at Natasha, then turned her around and pointed her in the direction of Sonja, who was still lost in what she was reading.

"Go and keep Sonja company till I get a break.

Unless you want to go and have a cosy chat with Matt instead, of course!"

Natasha glanced over at Matt, who sat hunched over the counter – suddenly engrossed in the menu that he must have known off by heart – and snorted.

"Ooh, I don't think so," she replied, making her way over towards the window booth.

Sonja looked up in surprise when she heard Natasha say her name.

"Hi!" she responded, as her fairweather friend slipped into the seat opposite her. "I didn't notice you arrive!"

"Mmm, busy, isn't it?" said Natasha, casting her long-lashed eyes around the packed room. "So what are you doing sitting here all alone?"

"Just hanging out," Sonja shrugged. "Seeing who else turns up. We all tend to gravitate here if we've got nothing else on."

"Well, what's your little chum Matt doing over there? Why isn't he keeping you company?"

"Oh, him," said Sonja, glancing over her shoulder at a shifty-looking Matt. "He's avoiding me, I think. Scared I'm going to give him a mouthful about all this secrecy rubbish."

"Serves him right if his girlfriend dumps him when she finds out he's been lying to her," said Natasha dryly. "He's such a loser."

"Aw, he's not that bad!" Sonja defended her mate against Natasha's derogatory words, even though Matt's behaviour was beginning to irritate her.

"Mmm," mumbled Natasha, unconvinced. Quickly, she changed the subject; she had no wish to fall out with the only friend she had in her home town. "Is my Uncle Nick in this morning? I haven't seen him in ages."

"No, not yet – but I think he's due in soon. So what's brought you home? You never really said last night. No brilliant modelling jobs on at the moment?"

Natasha's friendly smile cooled a little; she shrugged a vague response and glanced out of the window with a bored expression that seemed to defy Sonja to ask any more. Sonja fidgeted for a second and wondered where to take the conversation from here. She felt stupidly nervous and a little bit inferior when it came to Ollie's worldly and successful sister, even though they were the same age.

"Ha!" she laughed, trying to shift the sudden downturn in the dialogue with a recollection of an old conversation. "Do you remember that you once told me I could be a model?"

"Mmm," murmured Natasha, pulling the Sunday magazine over the table towards her and not responding to Sonja's eager smile. "Well, why not?"

Sonja was stumped by her indifference.

Natasha never shut up about modelling when we were hanging out before, she fretted to herself. *So what's up with her now?*

"Son – will the news-stand at the station be open?" Natasha glanced up from the shiny pages of the supplement.

What – so you can go and buy a magazine to read and ignore me some more? thought Sonja, irritated by Natasha's blanking technique. Nevertheless, she stretched out of her seat, leant towards the plate-glass window and squinted down the street towards the station.

"Yep, it's open," she said flatly, having caught a glimpse of the bank of colourful magazine covers that were stacked against the stand within the station ticket hall.

"Right," said Natasha, standing up to her full, willowy height – the eyes of most of the café clientele being automatically drawn towards her as she did so. "I'll be back in a minute. Ask Ol to get me a black coffee, will you?"

Sonja watched Natasha stroll away, tossing her silken brown hair back from her face and apparently oblivious to the stares from the surrounding tables. No one in the End was used to that much natural glamour with their eggs and bacon on a Sunday morning.

"I read somewhere that most models look pretty rough without the make-up and the lights," said Matt, reluctantly slouching on to the banquette next to Sonja and forcing her to budge up. "Not true in her case, though, is it?"

"Nope," she agreed. Natasha seemed to look great *all* of the time.

"So where's Winstead's own Kate Moss gone then?" he asked sarcastically, curiosity getting the better of his reluctance to sit with Sonja.

"The news-stand at the station."

"Pity. I thought she was maybe getting a train..."

Sonja couldn't help grinning at Matt's snide remark, but she slapped his forearm anyway.

"Ow!" Matt rubbed his arm, exaggerating the pain.

"You two are never going to kiss and make up, are you?" said Sonja unsympathetically.

"No," Matt responded, pulling up his sleeve as if he'd find an angry welt forming on his arm. "But she wouldn't let me anyway – it would smudge her perfectly applied lipstick..."

Ollie walked over to the table just as Sonja began to punish Matt's sarcasm with death-by-tickling.

"Where's Tasha?" he asked, ignoring his

friends' antics and plonking a mug of black coffee on the table. "I brought this over for her."

Before Matt and Sonja could stop breathlessly giggling enough to answer him, the door tinkled open and Natasha breezed back in, flopping down on the banquette and dropping a thick, glossy style-mag on to the Formica-topped table.

"Forgot that I did a shoot for this month's issue," she muttered, flicking through the fashion section pages, so engrossed that she didn't appear to register the fact that Matt had joined Sonja or that her brother was hovering beside them.

"There!" she said, slapping her hand on a double-page spread of arty black and white shots.

Ollie shuffled round and stood behind her for a better look at his sister's modelling moment. Matt and Sonja leant across, tilting their heads in unison to view the fashion photos. For a second no one said anything.

"My agency's going to love these," said Natasha, matter-of-factly, flicking over the page to the next batch of poses. "This photographer's worked with Christy Turlington, Eva Herzigova – the lot."

"Um..." Ollie bumbled finally, flicking his eyes across to check out Matt and Sonja's stunned expressions, "Well, I guess I don't know much about fashion, but—"

Nick, who'd just wandered into the café for his shift and was curious as to what was distracting Ollie from his work, ambled unnoticed over to the table and peered over their shoulders.

"Whay-hey!!" he bellowed inappropriately, before the terrible realisation dawned on him that the nearly naked girl he was leering at was none other than his own niece.

CHAPTER 4

●●●●●●●●●●●●●●●●●●●●●●●●●●●●●●

REFLECTIONS

"Son – hurry up in there!" bellowed Lottie's voice from outside the bathroom door.

"Use the loo downstairs!" Sonja bellowed back, annoyed at being disturbed in her tranquil magnolia-and-jasmine-scented bath.

Not that she was feeling very tranquil. She kept thinking back to the events of the morning and giggling at the image of Nick turning fire-engine red when he caught sight of Natasha's extremely artistic but terribly revealing photos.

"I don't need the loo – I want a shower! I'm going out tonight!" Lottie bellowed again.

"OK, OK – give me five minutes!" yelled Sonja wearily.

She knew that she wasn't about to rush and that it'd take her a lot more than five minutes to get herself motivated and out of there. But that was something Lottie would understand: in the Harvey household, everyone knew the rules: five minutes translated as fifteen minutes; "I'll do it now" meant "I'll do it in a little while"; and any insults – particularly between the three girls – were always (well, usually) meant in fun and never (often) taken seriously.

Sonja knew enough about her friends' families to appreciate she had a lucky combination in her own home: her parents ran a relaxed, unpressurised set-up, in an atmosphere that none of their children (hardly ever) abused.

Sonja twirled her toe absently around the cold metal tap and let her gaze rest on the uneven rows of moisturising body lotions, aromatherapy bath oils, hair serums, balms and hot wax treatments – all packed full of ceramides, keratins and pro-vitamins, whatever they were. The packaging on all these products made it seem like the bathroom had more nutrients on its shelves than the kitchen cupboard.

You can tell it's a house full of women, Sonja ruminated. *Poor Dad doesn't get a look-in!*

Her father's few toiletries were consigned out of sight to the pine cabinet above the sink, while his razor was nowhere to be seen – he'd taken to hiding it since all three of his daughters had an annoying habit of nicking it for their armpits and legs.

And if the traces of her dad's belongings in the bathroom were pretty marginal, there was no sign of Sonja's big brother Peter at all. But that was no surprise, considering he'd lived away from home for the last couple of years. Sonja's mother made sure he still had a room to call his own, though he'd been demoted to the smallest one in the house – Sonja having made a bid for his large room the moment he'd left it.

No trace... the words slipped into her mind. But she wasn't thinking of Peter this time – it was Owen's face that floated in the steam in front of her.

Sonja shook her head and the vision disappeared. She'd made a vow not to think about Anna's gorgeous big brother again; it hurt too much. It hurt too much to care for someone that madly, but never hear from him.

Sonja gave one final stretch in the rapidly cooling water and pushed herself out of the bath with a whoosh of water. Standing on the deep-piled bath mat, she stretched across to the heated towel rail and yanked a huge, fluffy towel from one of the bars. As she did so, she caught a hazy glimpse of herself in the steamed-up, full-length mirror on the back of the door.

A quick rub with the towel and the condensation was cleared enough for Sonja to take a long look at herself. She pulled the scrunchie out of her piled-up mop of blonde hair and let it tumble over her damp shoulders.

Studying her reflection, she knew she was pretty – and all thanks to her mum. Helena's Swedish background had given all four of her children the same colouring (blonde, summer sky blue-eyed, warm skin-toned). The only thing they'd taken from their dark-haired father was his height. Sonja was the shortest of the children at 1.8 metres and that made her taller than any of her girlfriends – unless you counted Natasha, and Sonja was still unsure how much of a friend she really was.

The conversation she'd had with Natasha earlier at the End was still preying on her mind.

What was with all that blowing hot and cold stuff? she wondered, turning this way and that in front of the long expanse of mirror. *Is Natasha trying to put me off modelling?*

Another thought came crashing straight in behind that one. *Or is she jealous? Doesn't she want the competition?*

Sonja smiled as the steam slowly encroached on her reflected image and decided that perhaps the time had come to get her own modelling career off the ground.

CHAPTER 5

● ●

SNAP DECISIONS

"Dutch?" suggested Anna.

"Or Belgian?" wondered Maya.

The two lads on the other side of the café stopped poring over the map spread out on the table between them, exchanged a few words and started to laugh.

From their vantage point in the window booth, Maya and Anna (who preferred to take her ten-minute break enjoying the scenery in the café than out the back with Nick) exchanged looks.

"What do you think *that* was all about?" said Anna, twirling the spoon around in her mug of hot chocolate.

"Maybe something like, 'Have you spotted those two really pathetic girls sitting ogling us?'" Maya grinned.

She was only joking. Maya knew that Anna worked the same way as her. When checking guys out, they both went for the subtle approach: quick glances when they wouldn't be seen, as well as acting as though they were so wrapped up in their own conversation that they hadn't even noticed Potential Talent's existence.

Of course, their whole cover would be blown the minute the other girls arrived. At the sight of the two very good-looking backpackers, Kerry would probably turn bright red and knock something over, while Sonja and Cat would try to outdo each other in getting the boys' attention – Sonja by zapping them into submission with those blue eyes of hers and Cat by heaving her bosom into battle station position.

"I wonder what's brought them to Winstead?" Anna puzzled, still trying to attune her ears to the language the lads were speaking above the sound of Radio 1. While the café was quiet and no one was putting money into the jukebox, she'd taken the small radio that Nick kept in the kitchen to listen to football scores and had stuck it behind the counter to try and create a little atmosphere.

"Bad map-reading skills?" shrugged Maya with a smile. "After all, living here's one thing, but I don't suppose the *Rough Guide to Britain* inspired them to take the train to the end of the line and land in gloomy old Winstead in late October."

"Actually, it's a pity those lads aren't Italian," said Anna, still stirring, although her hot chocolate was now less than lukewarm. "You could have learned a few phrases from them before you jet off there on Saturday."

"What, phrases like, 'I'm here on holiday with my parents, but please don't think I'm a loser?'"

"Are you really that bothered about going on holiday with your parents? I'll swap, if you want – I'd do anything to see Florence."

Maya felt guilty. Anna was only a little bit older than her, but she was having to take care of herself. Wages for an eighteen-year-old waitress probably didn't stretch very far – not to Florence, that was for sure.

"Sorry – I didn't mean to sound ungrateful about it. It's just that I suppose I'm at the stage where I'm feeling too old to be going on holiday with Mum and Dad and the kids. I'd love to go away with my friends, but that's not going to happen."

"Why not?" asked Anna. Being on her own was sometimes excruciatingly lonely and financially difficult, but she hadn't realised how much she'd begun to take her freedom for granted.

"My parents have only just started to loosen the leash with me the last few months, since we had a big bust-up in the summer," Maya explained. "I'm just grateful that they let me do the ordinary stuff these days, like going out on a school night occasionally. I wouldn't dare push it any further."

Now it was Anna's turn to feel guilty. In the short space of time that she'd properly become a part of Ollie's crowd, she'd never heard Maya moaning about her home life; she always seemed so together, so assured.

But Anna knew more than most what it was like to put on a brave face and hide your troubles away. After all, none of her new-found friends knew exactly what had made Anna leave everything behind in her old life and come to a sleepy backwater like Winstead. And she didn't know if her secret was something she would ever be able to tell them.

"Oh, look," said Maya, diverting Anna's attention to the street outside. "Here comes Kerry and Sonja. How about a bet?"

"What on?"

"How long it takes Sonja to find an excuse to talk to those lads."

"Right!" laughed Anna. "You go first."

"OK..." said Maya thoughtfully, "I'll bet you

that she's yapping to them within the next five minutes."

Maya and Anna both looked up at the wonky clock on the café wall, as if by some miracle it would actually tell them the right time, then realised their mistake and glanced down at their watches.

"Well, I'll say it'll take her closer to fifteen minutes," said Anna. "What are we betting?"

"How about 10p?"

"Oooh, I think I can manage that. Done!"

The door tinkled open and Sonja strode in, her shining, honey-blonde hair bobbing, apparently immune to the blustery wind outside that had whipped poor Kerry's curls into a mutinous bundle of frizz.

"Looks like you've been here a while," said Sonja, peering at Maya's empty coffee cup. "How come?"

"We got let out of the last lesson – Mr Stanley went home early with flu."

"Nice one," said Sonja enviously. "Anyhow, are you on or off duty, Anna? Who's serving?"

"Oh, I've just about finished my break. What do you want?"

"But we don't want to rush you, Anna, that's not fair!" Kerry chipped in, trying to smooth down her over-excited hair.

"Don't worry about it," smiled Anna. "Ollie's off tonight rehearsing and you'll die of thirst if you wait for Nick to serve you."

"What's he doing through there anyway?" asked Maya, peering behind the counter to the kitchen. "It's not like he's got any cooking to do. It's too quiet in here for that."

"He said he was going to do some 'tidying', which means he's sitting at the back door reading a music paper," smiled Anna knowingly. "But, yeah, you're right, it is quiet – there's only those boys over by the jukebox."

Anna gave Maya a conspiratorial wink as the other two girls swivelled their gazes around.

"Oh, yeah," said Sonja disinterestedly.

Maya's eyes met Anna's and a barely perceptible frown flitted across her forehead. Sonja? Not intrigued by these new boys in town? Was she ill?

Kerry was still squinting at them, when Maya noticed how red her eyes were.

"Are you OK, Kerry?" she asked, full of concern. She hoped those bloodshot eyes had nothing to do with her and Ollie yet again – there'd been too many tears in their relationship lately and they were only just supposed to have worked things out between them.

"Oh, it's just my contact lenses – I've never

worn them out on such a windy day," Kerry answered with a watery smile. "It feels like half of the kiddy park sandpit's blown in my eyes. Think I'll go and try and sort myself out actually..."

Scooting past Sonja's knees, Kerry made her blurry way towards the loos.

• • •

Kerry felt strange pangs of alarm that had nothing to do with the fact that one of her dust-encrusted lenses was playing hide and seek and had slithered somewhere unreachable under her eyelid. What had made her uneasy was her conversation with Sonja on the way to the End this afternoon.

Or, more like it, her nodding session with Sonja – Sonja talking fast and furiously while all Kerry could do was mutter a few useless "uh-huhs" and "ah, but"s in between.

The trouble was, Sonja had proclaimed that she was about to get into modelling. Seriously. There were four problems here, as far as Kerry was concerned.

1. Did this mean that Sonja was right back in with Natasha all of a sudden? Kerry didn't fancy going through all that losing-her-best-friend thing again.

2. Was Sonja getting a little big-headed here? Yeah, she was pretty – no doubt about that. But the way *she* was talking, it was a sure-fire deal that some agency would take her on. Wasn't that a bit presumptuous?

3. When Sonja got on one of these rolls about how *she* was going to do this and *she* was going to do that, she ended up sounding worryingly like her cousin. And frankly, one ego like Cat's was as much as Kerry could handle.

Finally, 4. Sonja's out-of-the-blue enthusiasm for this new project reminded Kerry all too well of her last hare-brained and ill-starred plan – the one where she decided that Matt might make good boyfriend material, even though she didn't fancy him in the least.

Kerry had managed to persuade Sonja out of this and had saved her from making a total fool of herself. But there was no guarantee that Sonja would listen to Kerry if things started to get out of hand this time.

Another thing that didn't seem right with Sonja was the way she never talked about Owen. Well, not since he'd left to go back to Newcastle after his fleeting visit to see his sister Anna a few days ago. Prior to that, she was always been wittering on about him. Now, she changed the subject whenever Kerry brought him up.

And it was *weird* her not speaking about Owen, considering how close he and Sonja seemed to have got during his last visit to Winstead... Kerry had never found out exactly what had gone on between Sonja and Owen after the impromptu party at Nick's flat. But Sonja had seemed so happy that Kerry had hoped that Sonja and Owen might try to make a go of their relationship – even if it was a long-distance one.

Retrieving the lens at last, Kerry clipped it with its partner inside her plastic carry case and splashed her face with water. She was quite glad she'd forgotten to bring her emergency back-up pair of specs – she didn't really want to see how bad her tangled hair and bloodshot eyes were.

With a head fuzzy with a jumble of thoughts and eyes fuzzy through lack of lenses, bumping into a backpack came as a surprise to Kerry as she made her way towards her friends.

"Oh, I'm so sorry!" said an apologetic voice, although it was Kerry's bumbling that had brought about the collision. The bulging nylon bag was made of such ferociously loud, luminous shades that it was as hard to miss as a double-decker bus in an airing cupboard.

An olive-skinned face rose into Kerry's line of vision and her automatic blushing response kicked into action, right on cue. It never failed.

"Are you OK? I shouldn't have left my bag there..." the boy said in a concerned, lightly accented voice.

"No – yes... I, um, I'm fine..." Kerry nodded, hoping her tumbling hair was hiding most of her flushed cheeks.

With a fixed grin, she steered herself towards the girls and flopped down with relief beside them.

"I'd like to believe you did that deliberately, as a ruse to get talking to those boys, but I don't suppose that's true," laughed Maya, trying to put Kerry at ease.

"If only..." mumbled Kerry, trying to tuck her unruly curls behind her ears.

"Anyhow, before Kerry distracted us by tripping into the arms of those boys," said Maya cheekily, turning her attention towards Sonja and playfully ignoring Kerry's indignant squeak, "you were saying? You want me to do some photos for you?"

"Yeah," nodded Sonja. "I want to send some shots out to agencies as soon as I can. But all the photos I've got are just so out of date, *and* they're all just snapshots."

Maya thrilled at the unspoken compliment: Sonja wanted professional shots done and she considered Maya professional enough to do them.

"No problem. We can both have a think about how and where to do them over the next week or so and then I can—"

"What?" interrupted Sonja, with an irritated note in her voice. "I haven't got time to hang around. They've got to be done this weekend. I want to get them sent off while I'm on half term!"

"I'm going to Florence for a week, remember?" Maya pointed out, slightly irked by Sonja's attitude.

"In that case, there's only one thing for it," shrugged Sonja. "You're going to photography club tomorrow, right?"

"Ye-es," Maya answered dubiously.

"Well," said Sonja brightly, "can you ask Billy if he'll do them for me?"

Sonja's hands were resting palms down on the table, but Maya felt as if she'd just been slapped.

CHAPTER 6

● ●

THIS IS YOUR LUCKY NIGHT...

"Remember to keep it down, lads," said Stuart Stanton, coming through to the back room of The Swan carrying a tray piled with cans of Coke and crisps. "The doors aren't lined with lead and I do have a pub full of customers on the other side."

"Thanks, Dad," grinned Ollie, taking the tray from him. "We won't go over the top – promise."

"It's brilliant of your parents to let us use this place to rehearse in," said Billy Sanderson, gazing round the sizeable room once the door had shut behind Ollie's dad.

The back room of the pub – host to Ollie and Natasha's seventeenth birthday party back in May – was set aside for functions. Often packed at the weekends, it generally stood empty during the week. And right now it was playing host to the first live run-through of the latest incarnation of The Loud.

"Well, my dad used to play in bands when he was younger, so he understands," Ollie explained.

"What kind of stuff did he play?" asked Billy.

"Ska, mod, two-tone – all that '60s stuff that was revived around the time of punk."

"Cool!" nodded Andy, his black hair slightly spiked in a not un-punkish way. "My mum and dad have never been into music – they just don't get it. They've only got about three tapes in the house and they never play them. Mind you, that's just as well; one of them's the soundtrack to *The Phantom of the Opera...*"

Andy stuck his fingers in his throat and made a retching noise.

"At least they're not going to do what my mum does," Joe chipped in. "She's always got the radio on and she sings along *all* the time."

"That doesn't sound too bad to me – at least she can't moan if you play your stuff quite loud," said Billy.

"Ah, but you don't know what she likes singing along to. Can I just say, Celine Dion and Mariah Carey?"

"Urghhh..." grimaced the other three boys in unison.

"That must be painful," Billy acknowledged.

"'Specially when she can't hold a note," said Joe wryly, chuckling at the familiar image of his mum, Susie, happily howling an unrecognisable tune above the clatter of the washing machine.

"Better not ask her to do any backing vocals for the band then, eh?" laughed Billy.

"You haven't heard *me* singing properly yet, remember," grinned Ollie.

• • •

Three hours later, two of the songs that Joe had written (although Ollie had to pretend they were his) and one written by Andy were finally sounding vaguely like proper tracks. They stopped and started, everyone fluffed different parts, but it still sounded half-way decent.

Grinning at each other with excitement, they decided to run through all three songs once again before they finished for the night. So caught up in what they were doing, it wasn't until the last chord of the last song faded away that the members of The Loud realised they had an audience.

"Yeah! Brilliant!" whooped Nick, clapping his hands as he moved out of the shadows at the edge of the room.

"How long have you been there?" Ollie,

breathless from the exertion of singing, asked his uncle.

"Long enough to hear you play three tracks – and they were great. Weren't they?" he said, turning to someone else in the shadows.

Natasha slunk forward into the light.

"Yeah, not bad," she shrugged, giving her brother a cheeky smile.

"Gee, thanks for your overwhelming enthusiasm!" Ollie teased back.

Nick's jeans were a little overly tight for his chunky thighs and you could practically hear the denim groan as he eased himself down to a perching position on Billy's amp. You could *definitely* hear Billy groan as he watched 15 stone of bloke make himself comfortable on his precious piece of musical equipment.

"Listen, lads," said Nick, pushing the sleeves of his leather jacket up as if he meant to get down to work. "I know a thing or two about the music business..."

Oh, here goes, thought Ollie. *Some old anecdote about him hanging out with the Rolling Stones again...*

"...and I think you've really got something there. Know what I mean?"

The four boys half nodded and grunted at the compliment.

"So I'm prepared to—"

"To what?" Ollie interrupted laughingly. "Let me off my evening shifts at the End – so I can rehearse more?"

He wasn't expecting what his uncle came out with next.

"To be your manager!"

The only sound that broke the silence was a loud clatter as Joe's drumsticks fell to the floor.

● ● ●

"So..." began Andy, staring across the table in the bustling front bar of The Swan at a morose-looking Ollie. "Does he know what he's talking about then?"

Andy didn't know much about Ollie's Uncle Nick, but he wasn't entirely convinced that a small town egg and chips-style café owner dressed like a *Stars In Their Eyes* replica of Status Quo could really do anything for them as a manager.

"Don't get me wrong," said Ollie, with a touch of urgency in his voice. His uncle had only been gone two minutes and he felt guilty for his lack of enthusiasm in front of the others. "I mean, I really like Nick – he's a great guy and a great laugh and everything. But it's just that he's..."

Billy and Andy stared at Ollie, waiting for him to enlighten them and finish the sentence. Joe stared at the table and didn't seem about to help out.

"He's just a chancer," said Natasha succinctly, her arms folded across her chest and a look of amusement on her face at the events she'd just witnessed.

"Aw, Tasha! That's not fair!" Ollie protested.

"Yes it is," she said defiantly. "I like Uncle Nick as much as you do, but he's still a bit of a chancer. All those endless stories about his days as a roadie, all the celebrity rock stars he used to hang out with... half of it's made up. If not more."

Ollie gaped at her cynicism. The other boys said nothing.

"But you've got to look at it this way, lads," Natasha said firmly, her model-learnt poise only reinforcing her position of control among the four boys. "What've you got to lose? Even if only a tenth of what he says about his past in the music business is actually true, it still means Nick knows a hell of a lot more than *you* do."

That particular truth took a second to sink in and before any of them could acknowledge that she had a point, Natasha was off again.

"So let him do what he can for you," she shrugged. "Then, if you get anywhere, you just dump him for a proper manager."

"The business woman has spoken," Ollie said dryly, looking at his sister, half in awe at the sense she made and half in shock at her ruthlessness.

"Natasha?" said Billy.

"Yes?" she said patiently, as if she was a primary teacher surrounded by a bunch of five-year-olds.

"*You* don't fancy being our manager do you?" he grinned.

"In your dreams..." she drawled.

CHAPTER 7

• •

DEVELOPMENTS

She was early. No one else had arrived yet at the low-built, breeze-block building that housed the photography club.

"Hi, Maya!"

Well, no one apart from Alex McKay, who ran the club.

"Hi, Alex!" Maya smiled at the rangy Glaswegian, whose long limbs spilled over the plastic chair he was sitting on.

Maya idly wondered what Alex's home was like; she imagined a Georgian flat, all high ceilings and elongated windows in keeping with his tall, skinny frame.

"What's new?" he asked, ticking her name off on his attendance list.

"Um, well, I'm off to Florence next week, so I'll

miss class, I'm afraid," she said, wriggling out of her jacket. "Or have you cancelled next week because of the holiday?"

"Nah," he grinned, looking and sounding for a second more like Matt or Ollie or Joe than a lecturer. "I'm not going away – just spent all my money on buying a flat, so I thought I might as well keep going for anyone who's up for coming."

Maya smiled to herself; his mentioning buying a flat right after her own little musing was one of those delicious coincidences that make you wonder if you're psychic.

"But Florence? Wow!" he smiled. "I hope you're taking your camera. It'll be brilliant this time of year – all moody skies and no tourists clogging up the view."

"Apart from me and my family!" Maya laughed.

"Fair point. So why are your folks taking you over there at this time of year?"

"My mother's friend from the hospital got a job over there last year and has been hassling her to come for a visit," said Maya, rifling around in her bag for the spool of film she wanted to develop. "I think this was just the best time for both families to get time off."

"Well, you'll love it, honestly," said Alex, with noticeable yearning in his voice.

Maya stopped rummaging in her bag and looked up at him. "Have you been there?"

"Oh, yeah," he nodded. "Spent three months there after college on a bursary. One of the best summers of my life..."

Maya sat down opposite him. *This* she wanted to hear; she'd read plenty about how beautiful Florence was meant to be, but it had all seemed too twee and Helena-Bonham-Carter-in-ruffles-'n'-lace for her to relate to. Now here was someone whose opinion she valued and trusted – no one else she knew was as down-to-earth and easygoing as Alex – and she couldn't wait to get his alternative real-life guide to one of Italy's most historic cities.

"Hey, hey, hey!" yelped a voice close by.

"Hi, Billy," she smiled tolerantly, the way she did when her little brother Ravi held up worms for her to examine.

Maya liked Billy a lot, but as a friend. He was just a bit too full-on for her to be anything more than that. They had dated just the once, but Maya knew straightaway that it wasn't going to work. Since then, he'd got so in with her friends so quickly that it had taken Maya a while to feel comfortable with the fact that he was around her so frequently.

"Hi, Alex. Brilliant – we're first here!" said Billy, yanking off his coat and bounding around the room with Tigger-like enthusiasm. "Are you developing or printing tonight, Maya?"

"Developing," Maya answered.

"Great – me too! Let's get in the dark room before anyone else arrives."

"OK," Maya responded, reluctantly getting up from her chair. She'd have much rather stayed and talked to Alex, but then this was a photography club – she knew she should take advantage of the equipment when it was free. And anyway, as soon as the others started arriving, Alex's time would be taken up talking technique and picture crops, not long-ago visits to Florence.

"What've you got to develop then?" asked Billy, once they were locked away together in the red-glowed blackness of the dark room.

"Just some shots of my brother Ravi and Kerry's little brother Lewis mucking around at the kids' play park on Sunday," said Maya, concentrating on loading the spool of film on to the big plastic roller which would then be immersed in developer. "What about you?"

"My headmaster asked me to do some photos for the new sports pavilion – y'know, shots of all the school sports teams in action, blown up big, properly framed and everything. Got some good stuff with the swimming team and the volleyball crew already."

"That'll be right up your street then, won't it? Your two favourite subjects – sport and photography – together," Maya said encouragingly, pleased that now he'd begun to concentrate, he wasn't bouncing off the walls with so much exhausting energy.

"Yeah," he nodded, his head bowed over a length of film he was extricating from the spool on the worktop in front of him. "'Course, you're forgetting my other favourite subject..."

For a second, Maya had the uncomfortable feeling that he meant her... But she was convinced that that was all over now and that he fancied Anna. (Though she knew, because Anna had told her, that Anna didn't fancy him.)

"Uh-huh? What's that?" she asked as casually as she could.

"Music, of course," he muttered, engrossed in what he was doing.

Maya let out a silent sigh of relief and fleetingly told herself off for vainly imagining that Billy still fancied her as well as Anna.

"You boys had your first rehearsal last night, didn't you? So it went well?"

"Yep – better than well. We've got ourselves a manager."

"A manager? How come?" asked Maya in surprise, looking over at his shadowy figure along the worktop from her. Not that she knew much about the music business, but she thought it would take a lot longer and much more work – gigs, demo tapes, etc – before a new band could snaffle themselves a manager.

"Nick's up for it. He caught the end of our rehearsal last night and loved it."

"That's great," said Maya dubiously.

She didn't want to burst Billy's bubble, but Nick? Sure, he'd worked with bands about a hundred years ago, but that was carrying their equipment about, not managing them. Would Nick know what he was doing?

"So it's been an amazing week," Billy said. "I can't believe my luck!"

Maya felt mean all of a sudden at being irritated with Billy earlier. No wonder he was walking two feet off the ground if so much was going right for him.

Which brought her round to something else that might make him pleased, even if it meant he'd benefit from her own loss.

"You sound pretty busy," she began, "but I've got another offer for you if you can fit it into your hectic schedule..."

"Oh, yeah?"

She could make out his figure straightening up and turning in the dark to face her.

"It's Sonja – it's for Sonja," Maya said hurriedly, worrying for a second that it might have sounded as if she was about to ask him out or something.

"What does she want? A foot massage? A signed photo of me?"

Even the dimness of the room couldn't extinguish the toothy whiteness of his ear-to-ear grin.

"No!" Maya laughed at his cheek. "She needs some shots done of her this weekend – she wants to send them out to modelling agencies. She wondered if you'd do them for her?"

"But what about you? You're her mate. Doesn't she want you to do them?" he said with concern.

"Well, yes, she did ask me, but I'm going away for half term," Maya muttered, the hurt suddenly rising in her chest again.

It wasn't just disappointment at not being able to do the shoot – it was more Sonja's tactlessness that got her. The way she hadn't seemed the least bit disappointed that Maya couldn't do it and had moved on to Billy without a moment's pause or regret. No "Aw, Maya, but I wanted you to do it!" – just a straightforward "Can't do it? OK. Next!"

It's stupid to let this get to me, Maya told herself sharply. *Sonja didn't mean anything by it.*

But although she tried to tell herself that, deep

down Maya wasn't entirely convinced. Sonja hadn't just been her usual tactless-but-harmless self the day before; she'd been very self-centred and – whether she meant it or not – mean.

"Whoo-hoo!"

Maya gazed up in surprise; she'd been so lost in her anti-Sonja thoughts that she forgot Billy was there for a second and couldn't think what he might be whoo-hooing about.

"Taking photos of a beautiful, no – *gorgeous* girl? Well, you just tell your friend Sonja that I just *might* be able to fit her into my schedule..."

Tell her yourself, thought Maya rebelliously.

CHAPTER 8

● ●

ANYBODY LISTENING?

"Hey, guess what!"

"What?" asked Sonja, without lifting her head from the *Yellow Pages* that she had propped open in front of her.

"Those two lads were in again!" smiled Anna conspiratorially.

Dorothy had just arrived for work and given Anna the chance to have a quick break. Since Sonja was sitting alone in the window seat with only the phone book for company, Anna had taken her orange juice and slipped into the red vinyl banquette opposite her.

"Which lads?" Sonja asked, without any real interest.

"You *know*! Those Dutch or Belgian boys or whatever they are. The two lads who were in here a couple of days ago! We were talking about them."

Sonja looked up at Anna, wrinkled her nose and shook her head.

"Nah, don't know 'em," she said flatly and dropped her gaze back down to the 'M' section she was flicking through.

"Yes, you do! Really nice-looking... Kerry tripped over a backpack of theirs. Maya and me were saying how we couldn't figure out why they'd ended up in Winstead of all places..." Anna tried to jog Sonja's memory.

But Sonja either genuinely didn't remember or she wasn't in the mood to even bother thinking about it. Anna hoped it wasn't the latter – there was nothing more infuriating than someone deliberately not getting what you were trying to say.

"Nope, sorry – don't know who you're talking about," Sonja muttered, her eyes glued to the page and her finger dragging down the printed words.

Anna took a couple of calming breaths and tried to give Sonja the benefit of the doubt.

"Listen, I was thinking," she began again tentatively.

"Mmm?" muttered Sonja. Her attention wasn't wavering from the phone book.

"I bought some new stuff for my flat this weekend..."

No response.

"Nothing flash – huh, like I could afford anything flash! Just a new rug and a throw for the sofa, that kind of thing. And I just thought it would be nice to have a bit of a girls' night some time soon. What do you think?"

"Mmm," muttered Sonja again, completely missing the significance of Anna's offer, if she had even heard it.

Anna's tiny flat above the End-of-the-Line café had been her own little retreat from the world since she first moved to Winstead. Even though she'd become friends with Sonja and the others, she'd never invited them all round before.

In truth, she didn't need a retreat so much now. She'd been longing to have her new friends around for ages, but it had taken quite a while to get the place looking decent. With a mishmash of rubbishy old furniture and fittings (Nick, her landlord, had furnished it with chipped, cheap second-hand gear) and no money to do much about it, Anna had felt too embarrassed to have anyone to visit properly.

But, after a few months of bargain-hunting and hiding what she couldn't replace under remnants of Indian cloth and old tablecloths she'd dyed vivid colours, Anna finally felt she had a home she could be (almost) proud of.

All of which passed straight over Sonja's self-absorbed head.

"So, are you up for it?" asked Anna, trying to get more of a response than just "mmm".

"Yeah, yeah, your place some time. Sure. No problem," mumbled Sonja. "Ah! Here we go!"

She pulled out a small pad and pen from her bag and started scribbling.

"What have you found?" asked Anna. She realised she wouldn't get Sonja's attention today even if she tap-danced on the table and screamed that Leo DiCaprio was walking down the street.

"The name of a modelling agency up in the city."

Anna watched Sonja write a name, address and phone number down. "Is this one that Ollie's sister recommended?"

"No – she only knows agencies in London and I don't want to go that far for work. Anyway," Sonja looked up and out of the window thoughtfully, "there's something up with Tasha at the moment. I tried to talk to her about modelling when we were here on Sunday, but she just acted really bored and disinterested."

Know the feeling... Anna thought to herself.

"Have you heard that this agency's good then?" asked Anna, wondering how Sonja had come to choose it.

"What do you mean?" Sonja replied defensively, looking directly at Anna for only the second time since she'd sat down, and for only the first time with any real animation on her part.

"Uh, well, I just meant, does it have a good reputation?" Anna tried to explain. "You know what they're always saying in magazines: always check an agency's credentials, in case it's dodgy."

"Oh, give me some credit! It's not like I'm writing off to 'Big Boobs Incorporated' or something. I am a bit smarter than that!"

Anna felt the cold stare of Sonja's icy blue eyes and wondered what on earth had got into her. Normally, Sonja was really good fun and always approachable.

"Well, sorry – 'course I didn't think you'd—" Anna started to apologise.

"You know something?" Sonja interrupted. "Since I mentioned this modelling thing, not *one* of my friends has had anything encouraging to say. Not Tasha, not Kerry, not Maya, and not even you."

Anna was stunned into silence by the accusation.

"If I didn't know better," said Sonja gathering up her pad and pen and shoving them into her bag, "I'd say some people round here were jealous."

Standing up, she walked away from the table

and shoved the phone book back on the shelf behind the counter.

"If you'll excuse me," she said dryly to Anna as she passed by the window booth on her way to the front door, "I've got to see a boy about some photographs."

Anna peered out the window and saw Billy and Joe crossing the road, heading towards the second-hand record shop next door. They, along with Ollie and Andy, were going to have a band meeting with Nick there at five, Anna remembered her boss telling her.

As she sighed and picked up Sonja's empty mug, it struck Anna that all Sonja's boy mates were about to get the low-down on her modelling ambitions, whether they were interested or not.

She hoped for *their* sake that they were more "encouraging" than she and the girls had been...

CHAPTER 9

• •

SONJA'S SECOND OFFENCE

"Yoo hooo!"

Cat, clattering along the path in a pair of ankle-strapped chunky sandals, couldn't see the tiny headphones that Sonja had slipped in her ears while she waited on the park bench for Billy and his camera to arrive.

Sonja, lost in a world of loud dance music to get her vibed up for the afternoon's photo shoot, couldn't hear her cousin caterwauling at her from along the rose-lined path.

"Oi!"

Cat's powdered and perfumed face loomed down right in front of Sonja's and made her jump out of her skin.

"Cat! Don't do that! You frightened me to death!" Sonja yelled too loudly, unable to gauge the volume of her own voice above the track that was belting out.

"Don't yell! Anyway, why are you sitting there in a dream with *those* blasting in your ears?" Cat chastised her. "I could have been anyone! A busload of perverts could have been creeping up behind you and you wouldn't have noticed!"

"What – at 11 o'clock on a Saturday morning with half of Winstead's happy families out strolling around and feeding the ducks? I *don't* think so," Sonja answered back at something more like her normal level, now that she'd pulled out the headphones and turned off her Walkman.

Cat huffily plonked herself down beside her cousin on the bench.

"And don't lecture me," Sonja continued, staring at Cat's cropped top, exposed midriff, cropped silky trousers and bare toes in her sandals. "Look at you: you're dressed like it's July. It's nearly November and there was frost on the ground this morning!"

"Oh, shut up, grandma!" pouted Cat, rocking one of her crossed legs up and down in irritation. "Just 'cause *you* don't keep up with fashion!"

"And what've you done to your hair? Is that supposed to be fashion too?"

Cat fingered the ends of her bleached-blonde hair, the tips of which were now dyed dark brown.

"D'you like it?" Cat preened, unaware of – or just plain ignoring – the sarcasm in Sonja's voice. "Alison on my course did it. It's really trendy at the moment."

Cat had started a two-year beauty therapy course at Winstead College of Further Education in September and seemed to spend most of her time trying out the treatments on herself.

"It's like having roots in reverse!"

"What do *you* know?"

"What I know is that if you're on your way to the End just now, you'd better be prepared to get the mick ripped out of you when the lads see that," muttered Sonja, pointing at Cat's bizarre new hair-do. "Try telling *them* it's trendy!"

"Is everyone in today then? Have you been down there already?" asked Cat blithely.

The sparring that went on between her and Sonja was such a long-standing tradition that generally neither of them took umbrage at any of the mutual sniping. Unless they were in the *mood* to make something of it – as their other friends had been witness to plenty of times.

"Yeah, but you'll just have Joe to speak to: Kerry and Ollie are being all lovey-dovey as usual, and Matt's there with Gabrielle. When I left, they were gazing into each other's eyes and feeding each other crumbs of carrot cake..."

"Yeurgh!" shuddered Cat. "And of course, Maya'll be off on holiday today."

"Mmm, lucky her," said Sonja enviously, looking down at her watch. "I think she said their plane was due to take off about eleven-ish."

Automatically, the two girls gazed up into the steely-grey sky and scanned the darting fluffy clouds for any sign of a plane bearing their friend away.

"So," said Cat, "how come you're here? And what's that?"

She nudged the well-packed sports bag at Sonja's feet with her chunky, sandalled foot. "Running away to join the circus?"

"*No.*" Sonja drenched the word in yet more sarcasm, widening her eyes and shaking her head. "I'm waiting for Billy. He's doing some shots of me – remember?"

"Remember? How can I remember? You haven't told me in the first place!" snapped Cat. "What photos? What for?"

Sonja suddenly realised she hadn't seen her cousin all week – Cat had been busy with a lot of course assignments and assessments (not to mention getting the tips of her hair dyed in weird ways).

"Well, I've decided to give modelling a go at last and Billy said he'd do some promotional photos of me."

"Yeah?" said Cat in surprise. "What got you thinking about that?"

"After talking to Natasha on Sunday," Sonja shrugged casually. "Do you remember her telling me once before that I could be a model?"

"How could I forget? I thought you'd given up on the idea until you left sixth form. So what now – are you going to approach agencies in London?"

"No. I thought I'd join something more local first, so I'm going to get in touch with an agency up in the city, once I get these shots done."

To be honest, Sonja expected a slagging from Cat as a matter of course ("You? A model? You must be joking!"), but Cat stayed uncharacteristically quiet.

"*So?*" Sonja pushed her for a response. "What do you think?"

Ignoring the question, Cat looked down at the sports bag once again.

"Got a few changes of clothes in there, have you?" she asked in a serious tone of voice.

"Yes..." said Sonja.

"Make-up? Got some make-up in there? Even though you don't normally wear much, you *do* need it for the camera..."

"Yeah, I know *that*," said Sonja irritably.

Cat tutted abruptly, folded her arms defensively across her chest and stared off in the opposite direction.

"What? What's up?" asked Sonja, wondering what had got into her cousin.

Cat's head whizzed round and she stared accusingly at Sonja.

"And what about me?" she hissed.

"What about you? What?" asked Sonja. "You're not making any sense!"

"Why didn't you ask me to style you?" snapped Cat, her bottom lip beginning to tremble. "It's only part of what I'm training to do – make-up, hair, looks... And I've always done make-overs on you all!"

Whether we wanted you to or not, thought Sonja darkly.

She hadn't deliberately avoided getting styling help from Cat – it hadn't occurred to her to ask in the first place. But Sonja didn't want to be her guinea pig for the day either. Being plastered with so much make-up that her own mother wouldn't recognise her wasn't quite what Sonja had in mind. And from past experience, she knew that Cat was capable of anything.

"Look, I never thought..." she began to say and then realised she'd made a mistake. By sounding half-way apologetic, she had given Cat hope.

"Then I still could be your stylist?" her cousin whimpered, her angry expression instantly

76

switching to little-girl smiles. "I could just nip home and get my make-up box and—"

"No!" interrupted Sonja, nipping Cat's suggestion firmly in the bud.

Back came the quivering lip, but Sonja only saw it for a split second before Cat stormed off down the path, her heels clack-clacking defiantly.

CHAPTER 10

• •

STRIKE A POSE

Sonja wriggled out of her combats, trying (unsuccessfully) not to trail them through the pool of water on the concrete cubicle floor.

Her sports bag was balanced on the loo (lid down) and, with her feet half-wedged in her trainers, she rifled about in search of her knee-length, blue chiffony sundress and cute little suede Converse mules.

I'm as bad as Cat – dressing like it's mid-summer, she smiled to herself.

Moments later, pulling the dress on over her head, the smile was wiped right off Sonja's face.

"Oww!" she yelped indignantly as her elbow grazed the rough plaster of the cramped cubicle wall.

"What happened in there?" asked Billy,

watching Sonja come out of the park toilets rubbing her elbow.

"Scraped half the skin off my arm trying to change!" she moaned, holding her arm out for his inspection.

"When I heard you cry out, I was going to come and see if you were all right," said Billy, looking at the slightly grazed patch on Sonja's elbow. "But I thought that anyone spotting me sneaking into the Ladies might think I was a bit dodgy!"

"'Specially since you're carrying a camera!" Sonja managed to grin.

"Right! Are you OK to do some more shots now? Or is your injury fatal?"

"Oh, I think I'll survive," she said, rubbing her hands up and down her bare arms to warm them up. "God, I bet real models don't have to get changed in grotty public loos!"

"Yes, they do. If they're doing outside shots, anyway," Billy informed her, rising to his feet. "I mean, sometimes they'll get a location van they can use as a changing room, but from what I've heard, often they have to get changed where they can – and that includes public toilets!"

"Hmm," Sonja responded, furrowing her forehead. "I think I'll stick to studio photo shoots when I'm modelling!"

"Hey, Son – don't forget that bag with all your clothes. You left it in there..." Billy pointed towards the small brick building behind her.

He was a little surprised by Sonja's last remark, he realised, as he watched her disappear back into the loos. She seemed so sure that she would be snapped up by an agency. There seemed to be no 'ifs' in Sonja's head: just solid 'whens'.

"OK, got it," she shouted, marching towards him, lugging the bag. "Where now?"

"I thought we could go over there," Billy suggested, indicating the nearby Victorian granite fountain. "You could walk around the edge, trying to keep your balance and stuff, and I'll just snap away fast. It'll look good – really animated."

Sonja was pleased with the idea. They'd done one 'look' already – Sonja in her combats and a long-sleeved fitted T-shirt chucking bread at the ducks – and she really liked what Billy was going for. The natural, unstaged look was just how she saw herself on the pages of her favourite magazines: no cheesy grins or posing-by-numbers.

She took the hand he gallantly held out to help her step up on to the wide rim of the fountain – even though she hardly needed it, considering it was barely a metre high.

"Thanks!" Sonja smiled down at him warmly from her newly elevated position.

She felt a flutter of excitement. The touch of Billy's hand had automatically kick-started the flirt reflex in her. It wasn't that she fancied him; not at all. He was quite nice-looking, in a sort of muscly, sporty way, but he didn't give her that little buzzy feeling she got when she was sure she liked someone *that* way. Someone like Owen...

But it's fun to flirt all the same, she told herself. *Just to prove I've still got it.*

"You can't see my bumps, can you? My goosebumps, I mean!" she laughed cheekily as she wobbled her way around the fountain.

"Nah, you're fine," answered Billy matter-of-factly, his face obscured by the camera.

"Oops! I didn't realise my strap had fallen down!" Sonja exclaimed, looking at her shoulder. "Should I, uh, just leave it like that?"

"Nope," said Billy, walking backwards as he snapped and ignoring her coquettish tone. "Looks like you're trying too hard."

Sonja pursed her lips for a second and hoisted the strap back up where it belonged. It seemed like Billy wasn't playing. She decided to change tack.

"So, Billy," she began mischievously, giving her blonde hair a little toss, "we've never had a chance to have a proper chat, just the two of us. You'll have to tell me all about yourself..."

"What's to tell?" he responded casually. "I play football every chance I get; I want to be a professional photographer – unless of course The Loud gets famous first!"

"Well," Sonja persisted, "what about girls? What kind of girls do you go for?"

"Come on, Son; you're smart!" he laughed, lowering the camera for a second. "You must know the answer to that!"

Does he mean me? she thought frantically for a second. *Has my flirting paid off that quickly?*

Then it came to her, lightning quick.

"Of course! " she exclaimed. "It's Anna, isn't it? You've been hanging around her loads recently!"

"Anna?" Billy replied. "No, it's not Anna. I mean, I did quite fancy Anna for a bit – still do, I guess – but she's not THE girl."

"Go on then," she teased, "who *is* the lucky girl? Is it someone at your college?"

"Nope," Billy shook his head and gazed straight at her. "It's Maya."

"Maya?"

Sonja was taken by surprise. She knew Billy had been into Maya when they first got to know each other at photography club, but they'd had one date that flopped like a punctured Lilo, and that had been that. They'd been nothing but friends ever since and both seemed quite happy to keep it that way. Or so Sonja had supposed.

"But you never act like you fancy her! You're always just matey-matey!" Sonja protested, stepping down off the fountain rim. This new revelation suddenly seemed much more important than posing for pictures.

"Son, I *am* her friend," shrugged Billy.

"I don't get it!" said Sonja. Whenever she fancied someone, she believed in letting them know about it.

"Well, maybe she'll fancy me back one day," he tried to explain. "But in the meantime, I'll settle for being her mate."

It was just about the saddest, most romantic thing Sonja had heard in ages – and it was real life, not some slushy video she'd rented from Blockbuster.

Billy spotted her sympathy-filled stare and started laughing.

"Don't go all soppy on me, Sonja – and don't feel sorry for me! I'm not going to be pining away in my room waiting for her to fall into my arms!" he hooted, throwing out his arms for dramatic effect. "I am willing to go out with any gorgeous girl who wants me, y'know, while I'm waiting!"

"What?" said Sonja, catching on to silliness, but still slightly disappointed that it wasn't some grand, unrequited passion she'd stumbled upon. "Some poor girl's got to be second-best?"

"Look," he winked at her, "you don't tell and I won't!"

"Deal," Sonja grinned back.

"Hey, look at you!" Billy suddenly exclaimed, coming over to her and putting his arm round her in a brotherly way. "You're shivering! Time to stop off for a coffee, I think."

Sonja let him scoop up her bag and lead her off towards the wooden booth by the lake that sold tokens for the rowing boats, ice cream, and – most importantly – hot drinks.

As they hurried over, it occurred to Sonja that she hadn't realised what a fun, sweet person Billy was. Or that she could be so jealous of Maya. *Or* whoever that second-best girl might be.

• • •

"I did think about asking Anna out just a couple of weeks ago – y'know, try to wean myself off Maya. But she wasn't up for it, I could tell and, to be honest, I was pretty relieved when I thought about it. Anna's a really cool girl and it wouldn't have been fair to go out with her and still be drooling over Maya."

Sonja – who was now wearing the entire

contents of her bag in an effort to get warm –
took another sip of hot chocolate while she
ruminated over what Billy had been saying. He'd
been totally honest with her; telling her how
thrilled he was to join The Loud, not just because
of the music, but because it gave him another
excuse to be close to Maya.

"Yeah, well, Anna wouldn't have gone for you
anyway – you're too young for her," she joked.
Teasing came as second nature to Sonja and it
was often the only thing she could think to do
when she didn't know what to say.

"Anyway, that's enough of my life story. What
about yours?"

"Mine? Well, let's see: my friends you know –
some better than others," she shot him a knowing
glance before continuing. "My family are cool,
apart from the fact that my older brother's
forgotten where we live since he moved out a
couple of years ago, and my sisters are horrible to
me. But I'm horrible back, so it kind of evens out."

"What about boyfriends, Sonja? Got anyone
special? Hey, weren't you seeing Anna's big
brother a while back?"

"No... no, that was nothing," she said,
skimming over the subject hurriedly.

Billy sensed he might have touched a raw
nerve and knew when to leave well alone. "And,

of course, you're into the idea of modelling," he responded, diplomatically.

"Mmm, not that I look much like a model right now, do I?" Sonja laughed, holding out her arms and regarding her odd but cosy outfit that included green combats, her blue sundress, a grey fleece and a black denim jacket hauled over the lot.

"Y'know, Sonja, modelling's not all that reliable a job," Billy tried to caution her.

"Oh, I know *that*. That's why I only want to do it for fun, not as a career. Long-term, I want to get into PR."

Billy knew he still wasn't getting his point across.

"It's like being in a band," he said, hoping she might just get it if he used a different example. "Like us in The Loud. I mean, we don't know how good we're going to get, but even if we turn out to have the potential to be the next Oasis or something, we might still not make it. We might still not be seen at the right time, or have the right luck, or have the sound that record companies want to sign right at that minute. You see what I'm saying?"

"Um, kind of," Sonja shrugged. To be honest, she didn't know why Billy had suddenly started talking about the band when they were supposed to be talking about her modelling.

"What I'm saying is, just because you *want* something doesn't mean you'll automatically *get* it," he said earnestly, hoping now that the message might sink in. Sonja was very pretty, but he wanted her to realise that it didn't mean contracts, money and fame were about to slip into her lap just like that.

"Don't worry," Sonja replied. "I'm sure The Loud will do really well."

She patted his hand patronisingly, then said brightly, "OK, I've warmed up now. Will we do some more shots? I'm never going to get signed by an agency if I don't have the right pictures!"

CHAPTER 11

• •

DON'T MENTION THE 'M' WORD...

"Got any haemorrhoid cream?"

"Ollie!"

Kerry widened her eyes at her boyfriend and glanced round into the pharmacy section of the chemist to make sure her boss, Mr Hardy, hadn't heard him.

"What – haven't you got any? You call yourself a chemist and you haven't got any haemorr—"

"Ollie, get out!" she shooed him away, trying not to encourage him by laughing. "I get my lunchbreak in five minutes!"

"OK, I'll go," he shrugged, pretending to take offence. "I know when I'm not wanted..."

Five minutes later, Kerry flew out of the shop and into his arms.

"You idiot!" she said as soon as their kiss was

over. "I nearly died! Mr Hardy could have heard you!"

"So?" he replied, squeezing her hand. "He couldn't have sacked you because I asked for haemorrhoid cream. And if he did, I think you'd find that an industrial tribunal would be on your side. In fact—"

"Enough!" said Kerry firmly, smacking her free hand over his mouth to silence him. "I only get an hour for lunch and I don't want to waste it listening to you wittering on about stupid haemorrhoid cream! Now, where are we eating?"

"Well, since it's a very special day—"

"Why, what day is it?" Kerry interrupted.

"Tuesday," shrugged Ollie, enjoying being silly. "Anyway, as I was saying, because it's a very special day, I thought I'd take you somewhere exclusive, rather expensive and with a truly amazing ambience..."

Kerry looked at the shopfront they were approaching in the High Street.

"But all you could afford was Burger King?"

"Got it in one!" he grinned, pushing the door open for her.

● ● ●

"I love having the money, but I wish I didn't have to spend my October break working," moaned Kerry, pulling back the top of her bun and dribbling a sachet of tomato sauce over her Spicy Beanburger.

"What – would you rather be sitting in the End listening to Sonja go on and on and on and *on* about her future in modelling?"

"Oh, God, she's not at it again, is she?" winced Kerry. Every time she and Sonja had met up in the last few days, every time they'd talked on the phone, there had been only one topic of conversation.

"Yep. Just as I finished this morning's shift, she arrived and started bending Cat's ear about it."

"Poor Cat..." Kerry said with feeling.

"Too right," nodded Ollie. "Cat came into the caff about half an hour before I left and was moaning on to me about how bored she was. But that's probably nothing compared to how bored she is now."

"Isn't Joe working at the End today?" Kerry asked, taking a bite out of her burger.

"Yeah, but he swapped with Irene so he's doing dishwashing duties, just so he can hide out in the kitchen and not have to hear Sonja droning on."

"What about Natasha? Has Sonja been back in touch with her? She told me she was going to give her a ring and talk to her about where to buy one of those books to put your pictures in."

"A portfolio? She's jumping the gun a bit, isn't she?" snorted Ollie. "She hasn't even got an interview with an agency yet, never mind any offers for work. But, whatever; I don't think she *has* been in touch with Tash. Not that Tasha seems to be in the mood to talk about work at the moment."

"Why? What's up with her?"

"Dunno, really. Nothing serious, I don't think. It's just that normally she's all 'such-and-such a designer says I've got a brilliant walk!' and 'ooh, I'm up for an advertising campaign job in the Bahamas!'"

Ollie's impersonation of his sister was spookily accurate, but Kerry didn't want to giggle in case he got defensive. He was very protective of his twin, even though they weren't particularly alike in personality.

"And this time she hasn't?" Kerry said instead.

"No, she's just been a bit quiet and mopey. I asked her to come along with me and meet you for lunch today, but she said she just wanted to hang about at home."

Kerry gave what she thought might look like a sympathetic nod. She wouldn't have wanted a moody, bored girl she had nothing in common with spoiling her precious lunch hour with Ollie.

"Hey, I forgot – this'll make you laugh," Ollie suddenly burst out. "When I was leaving the End, I heard Sonja tell Cat that she'd *never* do such a revealing shoot as that one Natasha showed us. Like anyone's begging her to!"

"What am I going to do with her?" Kerry mumbled helplessly through her food. "I've already tried to hint to her that she's expecting too much from this modelling lark and going on about it too much."

"That's the polite way of saying it, isn't it?" Ollie grinned, picking up a handful of fries. "Don't you mean she's turned into a big-headed pain-in-the-neck and she's boring the knickers off of all her friends?"

"Oh, Ollie, don't say that... It sounds so mean!"

"But it's true!" Ollie reasoned. "Listen, Kerry, I like Sonja a lot, but there are times – and this is one of 'em – that she's a bit too much like someone else we know for her own good!"

Kerry looked at Ollie and knew that they were thinking of the same someone. Someone who, at her worst, was vain, self-centred, thoughtless and amazingly annoying.

● ● ●

Right at that moment, Cat wasn't being vain, self-centred, thoughtless or amazingly annoying. Instead, she was doing something that was very, very difficult for her. She was trying to be patient.

"Y'know, it struck me last night – I really should learn how to drive," Sonja proclaimed.

"Yeah? What made you think of that?" asked Cat, glad that for the first time in twenty minutes the conversation had turned to another topic.

"Well, I just thought it would be handy to get to modelling jobs. You can get sent all over the place, you know. Which reminds me, I should ask my dad if I can have a mobile phone as well, just to keep in touch with the agency..."

Cat had been very proud of the way she'd forgiven Sonja for not letting her style her for the shoot (not that Sonja seemed to remember their last tense meeting on Saturday from the way she'd breezed in), and she was especially proud of the fact that she'd managed to listen to Sonja's boasting for a whole half hour, resorting to only the bare minimum of digs along the way.

But now she was ready to snap, and the only thing that saved Sonja was the bell. Not that she realised it, but the tinkling of the café door, and the entrance of Matt and Gabrielle, had distracted Cat long enough *not* to empty a packet of cheese and onion crisps over her cousin's head.

"Matt! Gabrielle! Over here!" Cat waved over to them enthusiastically as if they were long-lost friends she hadn't seen in a thousand years. And as if the last place they'd expect to see Cat and Sonja was in the window booth of the End-of-the-Line café.

"Uh, all right?" Matt grunted suspiciously. He always got suspicious when Catrina was being a little *too* friendly for comfort. His comfort, anyway.

"Gabs! Sit down beside me! How are you?" Cat twittered, patting the red vinyl of the padded seat.

"Yeah, I'm fine, thanks, Catrina," Gabrielle smiled at her. "Hey, I like your hair!"

Cat twiddled the brown tips of her bright blonde hair and shot a 'See?' look at Sonja. "Well, I love yours too! You must braid mine like that some time – and put in some of those dinky little beads! Wow – maybe you could do it next Wednesday, at Anna's girls' night!"

Cat's motives (this once) were totally innocent, but Matt wasn't to know that. Watching his conniving ex sucking up big time to his girlfriend filled him with dread. As did the thought of Anna's upcoming girls' night.

It was really sweet of her to include Gabrielle in her invitation, but the idea of Gabrielle being alone and unprotected in the presence of Cat made him feel slightly queasy.

Matt was concentrating so hard on figuring out what Cat might do next that he practically yelped when Sonja spoke.

"You haven't seen Billy the last couple of days, have you?" she asked.

"Um, no. Why?" he replied, still keeping a worried eye on Cat and Gabrielle.

"Oh, it's just that he did some shots of me on Saturday – you know, for my modelling? And I—"

"Right, that's it!" Cat suddenly announced, turning her attention away from Gabrielle and gathering up her bag. "I've got to go! Sorry, Gabs..."

"Where?" asked Sonja.

"Oooo – just somewhere..." said Cat enigmatically as she stomped out of the café.

"Just somewhere I can't hear your boring prattlings, you silly moo," she added under her breath.

CHAPTER 12

• •

BORED, BORED, BORED!

"Ollie, I'm *booooorrrrrred*!!"

"And I'm busy, so get lost, Cat," Ollie replied, without a trace of malice in his voice.

"No, you're not," said his friend, leaning her arms and her chest on the counter of Nick's Slick Riffs record shop and staring at Ollie pleadingly as if he could magically make something entertaining happen. "There's no one in here apart from me!"

"Just 'cause there's no customers doesn't mean there's no work, Cat," said Ollie, without lifting his head from the forms he was filling in.

"What are you doing then?" she asked, trying to pull the sheets of paper away from him and turn them around towards her.

"Cataloguing records," he said in a firm voice, pulling the forms back round to face him, "before

I price them and put them out in alphabetical order in the racks."

"Sounds just *fascinating*," sneered Cat.

"Well, it's just one of those things you have to do when you've got a thing called a *job*. You wouldn't know," Ollie teased her.

"You know something?" Cat sighed, oblivious to his cheek.

"Nope," Ollie responded flatly.

"This is the most boring holiday ever. It's Thursday already, the week's nearly over and I've done nothing!"

"Well, what are you bugging me for? It's not my fault."

"I know, but it's not fair. No one's around! Maya's away, you and Joe and Kerry and Anna are all working, and Matt's... well, Matt's just being wet."

"You mean Matt's doing something with Gabrielle," Ollie clarified.

"Same difference," shrugged Cat.

"Still, *Sonja's* not working – there's nothing stopping you hanging out with her..." suggested Ollie with a little grin.

"No, thank you!" barked Cat indignantly. "I'd rather dye my hair mousy-brown than spend any time with her at the moment!"

"Cat, your hair *is* mousy-brown underneath all

that bleach," Ollie pointed out, his eyes still glued to his figures.

"Exactly!" Cat responded emphatically and illogically.

"Guess I can't blame you," he smiled, raising his eyes at last. "Kerry's just about had enough of Sonja at the moment too. And I reckon she'll be worse today..."

"How come?" asked Cat, fiddling with the pricing gun in front of her on the counter.

"Billy was developing and printing up those shots of her last night. He told me at band rehearsal on Tuesday night that she'd arranged to meet him today to get them off him."

"What, next door?" asked Cat, thumbing her hand in the direction of the End.

"Yeah," answered Ollie. "Don't know what time, though."

"Well, that's it – I'm not hanging about in *there* this afternoon. No *way*."

"And you're not hanging about in here either," said Ollie. "If Nick and Bryan come back from this record fair and find that I've done nothing, it'll be dishwashing duty at the caff for me for the next year!"

Ollie's Uncle Nick and long-time buddy Bryan, who ran the second-hand record shop, were always skiving off on 'business', leaving Ollie in charge. Not that he minded; it was fun hanging out in Slick Riffs and having a legitimate excuse to listen to loads of records and CDs, instead of darting around in the hot, sticky café.

"But, Ol!" whimpered Cat. "What am I supposed to do?"

"Actually, it's a pity that you and my sister don't get on," he said, ignoring Cat's grimace at the mention of Natasha's name. "She's as bored as you."

"God, what's the catwalk queen doing still stuck with us mere mortals in Winstead? Hasn't she got to jet off somewhere and model Gucci bikinis or something?"

"Nope, she doesn't seem to have any work on at the moment," Ollie shook his head. "Now, Cat, don't you have to jet off and be bored somewhere else?"

Cat was about to reluctantly do as she was told when the creaky door of the shop was pushed open and Billy and Andy strolled in.

"Hi, boys!" trilled Cat, her eyes lighting up. Slithering around the other side of the counter beside Ollie, she picked up one of the albums from the pile that he had been sorting through.

"What can I sell you today? Can I interest you in this overpriced, outdated, scratchy record?

Or one of the other overpriced, outdated, scratchy records we have in this fine emporium?"

"I like your assistant, Ol," laughed Billy. "She's very enthusiastic."

"She's also just going, aren't you, Cat?" said Ollie, giving her a hefty nudge with his hip.

"Nope," Cat replied, enjoying her game. She picked up the pricing gun and clattered a ticket on to the album she was holding in her other hand.

"Mmm," nodded Andy, peering at the ticket. "You're right, Cat – it is overpriced in here: £4000 *does* seem a lot for a second-hand Madonna album when you can get a CD of it in Our Price for a tenner."

"Cat! It should be £4! What have you done?" Ollie sighed, grabbing the price gun from her hand and checking the setting that she'd fiddled with.

Cat looked suitably repentant, but before Ollie could shoo her away again, Billy spoke.

"Hey, have either of you seen Sonja around? I'm supposed to be meeting her in the café to show her these..." he held up a large brown envelope, "...but she wasn't in there a second ago."

"Are those her photos from Saturday?" asked Cat, her eyes narrowing. "Can I have a look?"

"Well," said Billy dubiously. "I really think she ought to see them first..."

"Oh, Son's my best mate *and* my cousin – she won't mind," said Cat persuasively.

Billy seemed on the point of giving in when the door of the record shop creaked open yet again.

Ollie was relieved, despite the fact that he needed to get on with his work. He'd just spotted that Cat had surreptitiously picked up a black marker pen from the counter and knew that he'd have had to wrestle it from her if Billy had let her get her hands on the shots. The mood Cat was in, Sonja would have ended up with a moustache and glasses scribbled across her face in lightning-quick time.

"Hi!" said Matt, walking up to the counter with Gabrielle in tow.

"Smells a bit funny in here, doesn't it?" Gabrielle commented, wrinkling up her nose at the permanent damp and dusty odour that pervaded the shop.

"Ah, it's all part of the atmosphere!" Ollie joked. "So what are you two up to?"

"We've just come from the city – there was a record fair I wanted to catch," answered Matt. He was always on the look out for new stock for his DJing business, even though he seemed to spend more money buying records than he actually got paid doing gigs.

"Wow, Matt, a record fair – *you* know how to show a girl a good time!" said Cat dryly. "Poor you, Gabs!"

"Oh, it was all right," smiled Gabrielle. "We went shopping too and he bought me this."

Cat looked at the intricately beaded choker that Gabrielle was pointing to, instantly felt jealous that she didn't have a boyfriend to buy her spur-of-the-minute gifts and promptly shut up.

"Anyway, we saw Nick and Bryan when we were there," Matt continued. "Nick asked me to pass on the message that they're going to be back later than they thought."

"Hey, big surprise," laughed Ollie.

"And he also said to tell you guys..." Matt looked round at Billy and Andy "...that he's got The Loud a gig. A really important one, he said."

"Where? When?" gasped Ollie, desperate for details.

"He wouldn't say," shrugged Matt. "Said he wanted to tell you lot himself."

"I'm looking forward to seeing you play. Matt's told me how brilliant your band is," smiled Gabrielle enthusiastically.

"Well..." shrugged Ollie, almost shyly.

"I'll bring all my friends to see you," Gabrielle continued. "They won't believe me when I tell them I know a proper band!"

"I don't know if we're quite a *proper* band yet," said Billy with a cautionary note, but looking none the less excited at the thought of playing an 'important' gig. "We're still just starting out—"

"But you are a proper band! Have you got a record deal yet or... or – groupies?" Gabrielle laughed brightly.

"Not us!" Ollie joked back. "Having groupies is more Matt's line!"

The realisation of what he'd said had *just* sunk in, and the resulting 'what-have-you-done?' pinch on his arm from Cat was *just* starting to hurt, when another creak heralded yet another visitor to the shop.

"Hi, Billy!" smiled Sonja, giving her other friends a cursory wave as she focused on the person she was most keen to speak to. "I just spotted you through the window. Are those my pictures?"

"Gotta run!" said Cat, disappearing out from behind the counter and grabbing her stuff in a nanosecond.

Although he was still reeling from his faux pas and aware of a throbbing pain from her pinch, it was all Ollie could do not to laugh at the sight of Cat pouting and pulling cartoon modelling poses behind Sonja's back before she disappeared out the door...

CHAPTER 13

• •

BARBED WORDS AND BAD MOODS

"Mmm – I'm not sure about this one; my hair looks too dark." Sonja squinted sulkily at the enlarged photo in front of her. The carefully wiped window table in the End was strewn with an assortment of colour images.

"Yes, a bit, but it's a great full-length shot of you," said Billy patiently, pulling out several more prints from the envelope he'd been carrying. "And anyway, in these two headshots, you can see your hair much more clearly."

"Hmm," said Sonja dubiously as she flicked through the photos. "I wish I could have seen the negatives and chosen the prints myself, of course..."

Andy shot Billy a look that said "isn't she being a bit ungrateful?" Billy replied with a quick "dunno" shrug.

Sonja, lost in looking at her own image, was unaware of the silent exchange.

"Well, there wasn't time for that," Billy answered her. "You wanted them turned round really quickly to send off today, didn't you?"

"Yeah, Billy rushed like crazy last night to get the negatives developed and print up the shots too – he had to phone and ask Alex if he would open up early just to get it all done!" Andy backed him up.

"And it wasn't as if I just chose these shots willy-nilly, I did get his advice on which ones I should print up."

"And Alex knows what he's talking about," nodded Andy. "Don't forget either, Billy here's an award-winning photographer!" Andy was talking about the competition Billy had won in the summer – with a photo he'd taken of Maya.

"Yeah, but winning a local competition and getting his picture printed in the *Winstead Gazette* doesn't mean Billy's gonna get *Vogue* or *Elle* begging him to do their next front cover!" Sonja laughed.

The fact that Billy and Andy weren't laughing back seemed to go right over the top of her head.

"They're good," said Anna, leaning over the table to look at Billy's handiwork as she passed by, tray in hand.

"Thanks, Anna!" grinned Billy.

"Mm," nodded Sonja, acknowledging the waitress's praise, but with a wary acceptance.

She still hadn't quite forgiven Anna for her lack of enthusiasm the previous week. There'd been a little frostiness between them the last few days because of it, but Sonja wasn't about to back down. Of course, part of the problem was that it wasn't just Anna who seemed to have a downer on her plans for modelling.

None of her friends seemed to be very interested or encouraging – not even Kerry. It wasn't that she'd said anything particularly negative, it was just that every time Sonja brought up the subject, Kerry always sounded slightly bored and started talking about something else.

Was I right before? wondered Sonja, thinking back to her sharp words with Anna. *Are they all a bit jealous of me?*

• • •

Anna turned away from the booth and scooped up a trayful of tomato sauce-smeared plates from the neighbouring table.

She'd heard Sonja's tactless comments about Billy's achievements and registered the two boys' stunned expressions.

What's up with Sonja at the moment? she wondered to herself, her powers of intuition failing to give her any clues. *Why is she acting so completely thoughtlessly?*

Anna too was still stinging from their conversation the previous week. She couldn't understand why Sonja had turned on her like that – apparently deliberately misunderstanding what Anna was getting at with her friendly advice. Anna had only *just* become friends with Ollie's crowd, only *just* let her defences down and started to trust people again, and the last thing she wanted was to fall out with anyone.

But, sensitive as she was, Anna was proud too – which is why she'd come to Winstead to make it on her own in the first place. And she wasn't just going to thaw out and pretend that everything was all right again. Sonja had no right to snap at her and expect her to take it.

What Anna *really* wanted was a chance to get Sonja on her own and ask her what all this was about. But the opportunity hadn't arisen so far.

Maybe next Wednesday, when the girls all come to mine, Anna suddenly thought. *Maybe I'll get a chance to talk to her then. That's if she comes...*

● ● ●

"What's up with you?" asked Ollie, looking over at his sister. She was flicking through a magazine so fast and furiously that the pages seemed to be crackling with her irritation.

"Nothing," snapped Natasha, glaring back at her twin, whose foot was drum-drum-drumming out an annoying beat on the living room floor. "What's wrong with *you*?"

Ollie glanced up at the clock on the mantelpiece.

"What's wrong with me is that it's 10 o'clock and I thought Nick would have phoned by now."

"About this gig thing?"

"Yes, about this 'gig thing'." Ollie sighed at his sister's lack of interest. "I'm dying to find out what he's got lined up for us, after that message he gave to Matt this afternoon."

"Don't get *too* excited," yawned Natasha, chucking her magazine to one side. "We *are* talking Uncle Nick here. It's not going to be *that* amazing, whatever it is."

"Well, we'll see, Miss Cynical! For all we know, there's maybe an A&R man in town—"

"Ha!" snorted Natasha. "A record company A&R man dragging himself from London to Winstead in search of new talent? I *don't* think so!"

"Tash, the world doesn't begin and end in

London, y'know! There are small independent record companies all over the place!" Ollie retorted. "And anyway, since Winstead's so dreary and dull to you, why don't you just disappear back off to your precious London instead of hanging around here looking miserable all the time?"

Natasha looked half surprised at her brother's outburst. He was normally so easygoing. But before she could answer him back, the phone rang in the hall and Ollie bounded over the arm of the chair to get it.

"Nick! What's happening?" she heard her brother say.

"Uh-huh... Yep... OK – when? Really? That soon? But who... Oh, go on! You can't leave it like that! Aw, come *on*, Nick!"

By the time Ollie got off the phone and sloped back into the living room, he had a grin the size of a planet plastered across his face. Pretending she hadn't been earwigging, Natasha looked up from the magazine she wasn't reading again and looked at him enquiringly.

"Nick's *only* set us up with a gig at The Bell next Saturday week. Guy Fawkes night!"

"The Bell? That dive of a pub?"

"Winstead's top live music venue," Ollie corrected her. The Loud (in an earlier incarnation) had played there once before, stepping in when another band had cancelled. Then they'd been doing covers of other people's records. This would be the first night they'd be playing their own music, in their own right, and with their new line-up.

"So what's so important about that then?" asked Natasha, referring to her uncle's mysterious message earlier in the day.

"He says he's got someone coming down to watch us – someone who could make a real difference to our careers!"

"Who's that? The noise abatement officer from the council? Coming to confiscate your gear for making too much of a racket?"

Ollie was too excited to rise to her sarky comments.

"He wouldn't say; said it would be a surprise."

"Wow! Then it must be the head of Sony records with a multimillion-pound deal!" sniped Natasha, all wide-eyed sarcasm. "I'd better iron your shirt ready for your appearance on *Top Of The Pops* next week then!"

"When did you get so bitter and twisted?" asked Ollie, irked by her attitude.

Natasha said nothing and turned back to her magazine.

"God!" Ollie blurted out suddenly, leaping

over the armchair again. "Got to phone the other lads and let them know the news!"

"Don't wish *too* hard for what you want," Natasha muttered under her breath. "It might not be what you expect..."

CHAPTER 14

ME, MYSELF, I

It had been a hectic Saturday morning so far. Most of Winstead seemed to have been struck down by colds and flu, judging by the amount of people who'd packed the shop asking for cold remedies, pills and potions.

Taking advantage of a late morning lull, Kerry got out from behind the till and set about restocking the empty shelf where the boxes of paper tissues were kept. There were a lot of runny noses in Winstead this weekend.

Crouching down, Kerry was lost in thoughts of Disney videos and Star Wars toys – it was her kid brother's seventh birthday in a week's time, and she still wasn't sure what to buy him for a present. She didn't notice Sonja until her friend appeared by her side, crouching down to her level.

"Guess what?" grinned Sonja.

"Owen's been in touch?" Kerry suggested.

"No," Sonja replied, her smile fading slightly. "No, I got a phone call this morning from that agency I contacted up in the city!"

Kerry's heart sank at the mention of modelling yet again; but seeing the excitement in her best friend's face, she immediately felt mean.

After all, I bored Sonny rigid about Ollie when we first started going out and she put up with it, Kerry reasoned to herself. *It's only fair that I should do the same for her.*

"Wow!" she gasped, hoping she sounded convincingly enthusiastic. "That's amazing. You've heard from them already? You only sent the photos off on Thursday!"

"I know. Brilliant, isn't it?" beamed Sonja. "They sound really keen!"

"Why, what did they say to you?" asked Kerry, standing up. Pins and needles were prickling her legs, and anyway, being upright meant she could check and see if the shop suddenly got busy. Mr Hardy was pretty easy-going and didn't mind friends popping in, unless his staff ignored customers for the sake of gossip.

"Well," said Sonja, straightening up too, "it was a bloke. He said his name was Anthony Jones and..."

Sonja was obviously dragging this out for dramatic effect.

"And?" said Kerry, playing along.

"And he sounded very, y'know, professional *and...*"

"And?"

"And he wants me to go to their office on Monday afternoon for a chat!" Sonja finally squealed, unable to keep up the pretence of cool any longer.

"That's brilliant! I'm really pleased for you!" smiled Kerry. Then a thought suddenly struck her. "But we're back at college on Monday."

"Yeah, well I reckon I can skip classes just this once," shrugged Sonja matter-of-factly. "The first day back after a break is never much of a full-on day. Even the teachers need to ease themselves back in gently, don't they?"

Kerry had never skived a day in her life; skipping a study period was as daring as she'd ever been in that department. She'd wanted to bunk off plenty of times, but her weighty sense of guilt never allowed her to.

But now she felt guilty for a different reason – guilty for being a lousy friend. In the face of Sonja's excitement, she felt gloomy as she remembered how much she'd been slagging her friend off to Ollie lately. It was time she made it up to her.

"Sonja?" said Kerry in a low voice, her heart pitter-pattering at the rebellious idea in her head. "It's just a thought... but what if I skip college too? I could come along and keep you company!"

She was completely taken aback when Sonja unexpectedly burst out laughing at her suggestion.

"Come on, Kerry!" smirked Sonja. "I'm not exactly eight years old! I don't *need* anyone to hold my hand!"

Kerry was relieved to see two boys walk into the shop at that precise moment. She could feel the heat of a blush stealing across her cheeks – caused by anger and indignation at Sonja's tactless words – and she didn't know how to respond.

"'Scuse me," she muttered in Sonja's direction before she stomped off to take up her position behind the counter.

Serving the boys took a few minutes; they were foreign and weren't sure how to ask for plasters in English. It was only when one of them pointed to his ankle and explained that his boot was hurting that Kerry clicked they were talking blisters. She'd probably have understood them a lot more quickly if her mind hadn't been fizzing with frustration.

For all her earlier thoughts of regret, it was now apparent that she'd been right in the first place. Sonja *was* behaving like Cat at her worst, and she *was* being completely self-centred and obsessive about this modelling stuff. In fact, Sonja was so self-absorbed that she hadn't even noticed that she'd offended her best friend and was blithely checking out the make-up stand till Kerry was free again.

"They were quite cute," Sonja said casually as the two lads made their way out.

Kerry looked at them as they passed the window and suddenly remembered where she'd seen them before. They'd been in the End the week before last; she'd tripped over one of their backpacks.

"They're the lads Anna and Maya were eyeing up in the café not so long ago. Remember?" Kerry prompted her, wondering if Sonja would pick up the new cool tone in her voice.

"Nope," shrugged Sonja disinterestedly.

She wants to get back to talking about herself again, sensed Kerry. *But let's just try something out – let's see if I can get her off the subject.*

"Speaking of Anna, her girls' night on Wednesday should be a laugh, shouldn't it?" said Kerry, picking up her boxes of tissues and starting to fill the shelf once again.

"Dunno about that," sniffed Sonja. "Anna's been a bit funny with me. Did I tell you?"

"No," replied Kerry, intrigued.

"Mmm, well, she started trying to give me a lecture about the perils and pitfalls of modelling or something," said Sonja animatedly, full of righteous indignation. "But I think she's basically just jealous."

Kerry almost felt like laughing – Sonja just *couldn't* manage to make it through a sentence without using the 'm' word.

Brushing past that topic, Kerry tried again.

"Maya's back tomorrow. It'll be great to hear about her holiday, won't it?"

"Yes. I can't wait to show her the photos Billy did of me!"

Kerry gritted her teeth and decided to give her friend one last chance to change the subject.

"Next Saturday is Lewis's birthday. We're going to give him a party and then take the kids along to the fireworks in the park since it's Bonfire Night too."

This was a real tester; Sonja was very fond of Lewis. She and Kerry had been friends for ever and they'd both gone up to the hospital together to coo over the bundle of pink baby that was Lewis the day after he was born.

"Hmm? Sorry, what did you say?" asked Sonja, her mind wandering off to somewhere more glamorous.

"Nothing," muttered Kerry, realising she was totally wasting her time.

CHAPTER 15

• •

GREAT EXPECTATIONS

There, that must be it! thought Sonja as she turned into the busy street. Ahead of her, half-way along the road, was an impressive, mirrored glass and red-brick building.

Architect-designed spaces, state-of-the-art interiors, staff who looked not *that* far off being models themselves: Sonja had seen it all before in her favourite magazines, in the sort of behind-the-scenes of major London modelling agencies that they regularly featured. Oh, yes, Sonja knew what to expect.

'Barnes & Partners Accountants' said the brass plate beside the front door of the impressive modern building.

That can't be right! frowned Sonja, reaching into her coat pocket and retrieving the piece of paper on which she'd scribbled down the address. *So, 49 Red Lion Street...*

She looked back up at the doorway in front of her and searched for a number. There it was... 39. She still had a way to go.

Turning, her spirits sank when she glanced at the row of ordinary shops that ran along the remaining length of the street. Nothing looked as promising as the building she'd mistakenly stopped at.

"41..." she counted under her breath, passing a betting shop. Number 43 was a neighbouring door that had to lead to the property above.

"45..."

A vacuum repair shop, flanked by another uninspiring door to somewhere.

"47..."

A hardware shop, with its contents of tackily-coloured plastic buckets and mops spilling out on to the pavement, almost blocking Sonja's path.

And there: number 49 Red Lion Street. A plain brown door with a row of grubby bell pushes to the right of it.

Sonja tried to swallow her disappointment and turned her attention to the names under each of the three black and white bell pushes.

"Doggy Locks Luxury Grooming Parlour..." she muttered, reading the top name. "Destiny Awaits

Dating Agency... Ah, here we go – First Call Models!"

She pressed the appropriate buzzer and waited for a response, her heart pounding. All of a sudden, Sonja wished she'd said yes to Kerry's offer of company today.

"Hello?" said a scratchy female voice via an intercom.

"Hi! This is Sonja Harvey – I have an appointment with Anthony Jones at 2.00 pm?"

"Oh, yes; come on up. First floor."

The door clicked open and Sonja walked into a small hallway with a scattering of uncollected junk mail on the floor. A clatter of footsteps and whining coming from the stairwell made her jump. Suddenly, a stressed-looking old English sheepdog with an equally stressed-looking owner came rushing down the steps. They fled out of the still-open front door, leaving behind the sickly sweet smell of dog shampoo and slightly burnt hair, before the door banged shut with a wall-juddering thud.

Stepping on to the scuffed stairs, Sonja noted with annoyance that her long, black winter coat was covered in white hair where the traumatised dog had brushed past her. Tutting to herself, she tried to flick away the worst of it, without much success.

She'd taken such care to wear the right thing

too, spending her Sunday scanning piles of magazines for one particular feature she remembered, where a model was photographed as she went about her work for a day. Sonja had found it at last and tried to copy the look as closely as she could: black zip-up ankle boots, natural-coloured tights, a short, grey skirt and a fitted black polo-neck top. Her only concession to the biting cold wind was her long coat; the coat that now had an unwanted furry trim.

Thinking fast, Sonja hauled it off and carried it over her arm as she continued her climb up to the first floor.

"Come in!" said the same voice that had answered the intercom.

Sonja tentatively peered around the office door and saw a middle-aged woman sitting behind a chipped wooden desk, a phone clamped to her ear with one hand and a cigarette held in the other. She motioned Sonja over to one of the low, beige, vinyl-covered seats by the wall.

Glad of the few seconds' break to take in her surroundings, Sonja scanned the bare white walls of the office. The only sign that identified it as a modelling agency was a lone 'First Call Models' sticker on the grey filing cabinet.

"Mmmm, I *know*. That's what *I* said," murmured the woman into the receiver.

Sonja found her gaze riveted to the woman's badly dyed, jet-black hair, its tonged curls held rigid by hairspray.

"Yes, I *know*. I heard that *too*," she nodded to the invisible caller down the line. "And then she said to me, 'June,' she said, 'you were right all along'—"

At this point, Sonja shuffled in her chair and gave a surreptitious cough. This conversation could drivel on for ages and Sonja was too keen to meet the guy she'd spoken to on Saturday morning to listen to any more discussion of some unknown person's private life than she had to.

"Mmm, hold on, Arlene, I've got someone in the office," said the woman, throwing Sonja an icy glare. "I'll call you back in a minute."

Sonja hid her victorious smile while the receptionist buzzed through to another office.

"Tony? There's a Sonja Hardy to see you."

"Harvey, it's Sonja *Harvey*," Sonja tried to correct the woman – to no avail; she was already dialling out a number that would no doubt reconnect her interrupted call.

A door on the far side of the small office was pulled open and a smiling, fiftysomething man in a V-neck Pringle jumper and slacks came striding across to her, his hand held out ready to shake hers.

"Sonja, Sonja, Sonja! Good to meet you at last! I'm Tony – come on through to my office!"

Perching herself on another beige vinyl chair, Sonja gave the room a two-second once-over and sussed out that it was a carbon copy replica of the room she'd just left – minus the frosty presence of 'June'.

"So! Sonja! Find us all right, did you?" asked the man who'd introduced himself as Tony.

"Uh, yes. Yes I did, thanks," smiled Sonja, omitting the part about her disappointment in the location of the agency.

"Great stuff!" said Tony breezily.

With his thick moustache and chunky gold neck chain, he didn't exactly fulfil Sonja's image of an agency booker either.

"Right! Let's get down to business! You want to be a model then?" he asked, reaching down into a desk drawer and pulling out a familiar brown envelope.

"Well, yes. I—"

Sonja was just about to launch into her well-rehearsed spiel about how she wanted modelling just to be a sideline; how she would be free to work only at weekends and during holidays, when she was stopped short.

"Fantastic!" Tony said over the top of her words, pulling her photos out of the envelope.

"And after looking at these, and seeing you here now, I can certainly see that we could do some business together!"

"Do you think so?" replied Sonja, softening despite herself at his complimentary enthusiasm.

"Oh, yes!" he nodded, his bushy eyebrows shooting up his forehead for added emphasis. "Lots of work, a beautiful girl like you."

"What kind of jobs do you get?" Sonja managed to ask without interruption. Even though she'd shouted Anna down for suggesting it, she did want to make absolutely sure that this wasn't a "take-your-top-off-and-stick-your-chest-out-love" type place.

"Fantastic stuff! Advertising work – lots of dosh in that, let me tell you. Catwalk shows, editorial work like newspapers and magazines – the lot. The girls and boys on my books get plenty of work, mark my words!"

Sonja was instantly relieved.

"Well, that sounds—"

"Yes! And you can be part of it, Sonja!" boomed Tony.

"Um, well, I'd love to—"

"Fantastic!" he boomed again. "I think we can have you out doing castings as soon as you like – once we get you some proper photos done for your portfolio!"

"Proper photos? But I thought—"

"These?" said Tony, pointing to Billy's pictures. "Nice work, but nah – not right for taking to clients. Too arty. But don't worry – got a studio here. We can get you in front of the cameras soon as you like!"

"I, um, well..." Sonja bumbled, totally thrown by the forcefulness of the man sitting opposite her.

"You're at school, yeah?"

"Well, sixth form, normally, yes. I mean, today I—"

"So how about next Saturday? I don't usually do much beyond a bit of paperwork at weekends, but it wouldn't be too difficult. What d'you say?"

"I guess that would be—"

"Fantastic! Great to have you on board, Sonja!" barked Tony, rising to his feet and ushering her towards the door. "Let me see... about four-ish? Got to take the wife to Tescos first, you know how it is."

"Four-ish? Oh, OK," nodded Sonja, finding herself propelled past June – who was still nodding away to her phone friend – over to the door.

"I'll get June to sort out the paperwork this afternoon; contract, details of commission," bellowed Tony with an ear-to-ear smile. "Cost of the photo session, joining fee, that type of thing. You know?"

"Cost of photo? Joining fee? But I thought—"

"Nothing to worry about. You'll make up the money in work in no time. Mark my words," smiled Tony, now standing in the doorway and waving her off down the stairs. "Till next Saturday, then. Fantastic. Bye!"

In the silence of the dusty stairwell, staring at the firmly shut door, Sonja's foot hovered uncertainly above the top step. Her head was reeling from the super-speedy meeting and she didn't know what to think.

But one thing's for sure, she finally reassured herself as she turned to descend the staircase, *I'm on my way to being a model!*

CHAPTER 16

● ●

TRUE LOVE AND HURTFUL TRUTHS

Matt was over the moon. Right at that moment, he'd have loved to close his eyes and indulge in the luxury of daydreaming about Gabrielle. But he couldn't – driving with your eyes shut was against the law, he was pretty sure.

Having just dropped Gabrielle off, Matt was in no mood to head home and hang about aimlessly in his huge empty house. His head was buzzing too much for that; he needed to speak to someone, to tell them that his heart was aching with happiness.

But who to tell? It couldn't be Ollie or Joe – it was Tuesday night and the band would still be mid-rehearsal. And it would be a full-on rehearsal now that they had their first gig lined up for Saturday.

Anyway, he wasn't sure if he'd feel quite right blabbing his emotions out to the lads: this confession needed to be heard by a girl. A girl would get it. A girl would understand why his head felt floaty light with joy.

Matt flipped on his indicator and turned off towards Sonja's.

• • •

With a house full of girls perfectly capable of looking after themselves (they hoped) Sonja's parents regularly took advantage of their freedom and disappeared off for long weekends and midweek breaks.

This time, the destination had been France and all three Harvey daughters were clustered round their parents and their luggage, each one of them as expectant as any little kid in search of holiday goodies.

As caught up as her sisters in this welcome home ceremony, Sonja was slightly irritated to see Matt's car draw up outside the house, under the yellow glare of the street light.

"C'mon in," she beckoned him, opening the door before he'd got as far as the bell. "Sorry about the racket – Mum and Dad just got back from a week in Paris."

"Oh, I don't want to interrupt!" said Matt, automatically starting to back away.

"Don't be silly!" smiled Sonja, her good humour and manners coming back at the sight of her friend's embarrassed shuffling. Matt always turned into a bumbling small boy in the presence of Sonja's noisy, massed family. "Look, we'll go up to my room. I can catch up with the folks later."

"I haven't seen Maya since she got back from Florence. Did she have a good time?" asked Matt, following Sonja up the stairs.

"Don't know," said Sonja over her shoulder. "I haven't been in the End the last couple of nights."

"What about college? Haven't you seen her there?" he asked, walking into her room and plonking himself down on to the padded velvet window seat.

"Nope, not today. And I didn't go in yesterday."

"Oh. Why not?"

"Well," answered Sonja, flopping down on her bed with a little smirk on her face, "I was up in the city – I had an interview with a modelling agency!"

"Yeah?" Matt responded. "And?"

"Mmm, they want to take me on!"

"That's really great," he nodded, with a glazed expression on his face.

Sonja noticed the way he was fidgeting manically with his car keys and had the impression that he wasn't totally listening to what she was saying.

"Something up, Matt?" she asked irritably. There was nothing more annoying than having someone ignore you when you were talking, she realised. Especially when your news was so exciting.

"Oh, Son! I had to come and talk to you! I can't believe it!" he grinned.

"What?" she asked, suddenly curious, and wondering what had made Matt lose his cool quite so much.

"Tonight, when I was dropping Gabrielle off, I... well, I told her I loved her!"

Sonja stared at him for a second.

"So?" she shrugged finally.

"What do you mean, 'so'?" he frowned at her. "Son – I told her I loved her! Do you know how that *felt*?'

"Yeah, but it's no big wow, is it?" said Sonja without a trace of tact.

Matt stared at her, dumbstruck.

"Well, you've told us often enough that you're in love with her, haven't you?"

"I know *that*," he blustered, his face pink with embarrassment and annoyance. "But the thing is,

I never had the courage to tell *her* before! And then..."

Matt's face came over all cherubic for a second and he shook his head as if he couldn't quite believe what he was going to say next.

"...she told me she loved me back!"

"Well, whoopee," shrugged Sonja, sweeping over her friend's emotions with one offhand remark. "It's very nice and all, Matt, but it's no big surprise. I mean, it's been obvious from Day One that you two have been nuts about each other."

Matt gripped his car keys silently for a second. He'd expected some whooping and hollering at this point; maybe some hugs and I'm-so-pleased-for-you tears. This sarcastic response wasn't what he'd hoped for from Sonja. Cat maybe, but not Sonja.

"Son – have you listened properly to anything I've been saying?" he barked at her, his self-consciousness at pouring out his emotions now turning to anger.

"Matt – did you bother to listen to what *I* was saying about my modelling before you interrupted me with all this 'ooh, she wuvs me' stuff?" she responded.

Sonja hadn't meant to come out with it quite that bluntly, but once the words were out, the damage was done.

"Right," said Matt, his face a mixture of hurt and rage, "I won't bore you any more! I'm sure you've got better things to do than listen to me – like get your moustache waxed before your next photo shoot!"

And, with that, he stormed out of her room and hammered his way down the stairs and out of the house.

• • •

Her father was watching the 9 o'clock news and catching up with a week's worth of happenings, Lottie was gabbing away on the phone to a friend, Karin was lazing in a bath filled with something that smelled expensive and herby from France, and Sonja was enjoying having her mother to herself.

Her mum was cool. At least she'd be excited by Sonja's news. Both her parents were keen for their children to be successful and happy in whatever they chose to do.

But the conversation was not going as Sonja had expected.

"Hold on a sec!" Helena Harvey interrupted her daughter's update "You mean you've already been to see this agency?"

"Uh-huh, I went yesterday. They said—"

"But, Sonja, college started back yesterday, didn't it?"

"Well, yes, but..." Sonja grinned at her mum. Both her parents were laid-back enough not to mind the odd bit of liberty-taking on the part of their children.

"Sonja, I'm not very happy about this," her mother stunned her by saying. "I don't like the idea of you bunking off college just like that."

"Don't worry – I caught up on all my notes and stuff today. I just copied them off people in my classes. It's no big deal," Sonja tried to appease her.

"Sonja, I think it is quite a big deal. You know your dad and I let you all have plenty of leeway, but you don't do something major like this without running it by us first!"

"But you weren't here!" Sonja whined. "What could I do?"

"What could you do?" repeated her mother, looking more stony-faced than Sonja could ever remember. "What about put it off for a while, till we came back?"

"But why? It wasn't like I was doing anything dodgy!"

"No? Going off to some office in a back street in the city – alone – is sensible, is it? Sonja, for God's sake, anything could have happened to you!"

"But, Mum!" Sonja protested. "It wasn't sordid or anything; it's a proper agency!"

"Well, maybe it is," said her mother with a frown. "But you didn't know that before you went. You put yourself in real danger – you could have been in trouble and no one would have known!"

Sonja felt prickles of indignant hot tears come to her eyes. Putting it like that, she realised that her mum had a point, but her pride wasn't about to let her admit it.

"Mum! Why are you talking to me like this? Why are you talking to me as if I'm some stupid, irresponsible little kid?"

"Because you've behaved like one, Sonja," she was shocked to be told.

CHAPTER 17

• •

SOMEONE LETS SLIP

Anna straightened up the cushions on the sofa for the sixteenth time, decided they looked too formal and mussed them all up again.

Next, she turned her attention to the walls where she'd just hung some pictures – made from greeting cards she'd stuck in cheap clipframes – and tried to work out if they were hanging squint or not.

Too bad if they are, she sighed to herself, knowing that the girls could turn up at any minute.

Right on cue, the doorbell went and in tripped Cat, cooing at how prettily Anna had done the place up since she'd last seen it when she'd given Anna a stunning make-over a few weeks ago.

"You've done the walls too!" Cat noticed,

stroking the formerly floral speckled wallpaper that was now painted a cool, relaxing, pale leaf green.

"Mmm – I did it on Monday. I had a day off," beamed Anna, enjoying showing off her newly-improved home. She was totally broke now, especially with buying food and drink for the evening on top of everything, but it was worth it. "I didn't tell Nick that I was decorating the flat – do you think he'll mind?"

"Mind?" laughed Cat. "I guarantee that you could plonk him down on that sofa and he wouldn't even *notice*!"

Nick's flat in the next-door building was a straightforward two-bedroom affair, but it was much grander than Anna's little garret above the café. From what Anna had seen of his flat (comfortable but stuck in a '70s time warp) she realised that Cat was probably right.

The girls heard a "yoo-hoo!" from the courtyard behind the café and opened the door to see Kerry on her way up, her smiling face hidden behind a large, bushy jasmine plant, as she carefully climbed the open metal stairs to Anna's front door.

"I know you've lived here for ages, Anna," she panted as she reached them, "but this is a bit of a flat-warming present anyway!"

Inside, Anna tried positioning the plant on the windowsill and was just asking the other two for their opinion when she spotted Matt's car pull up outside.

"Here comes Gabrielle," she said to the others.

"Look at that," said Cat with her usual edge of sarcasm, peering out at the blue Golf. "He's such a gentleman he's even escorting her here!"

"It's a wonder he's even letting her out of his sight!" Kerry joked, conveniently forgetting how claustrophobically inseparable she and Ollie had been in the first few weeks of their relationship.

"I wouldn't be surprised if he's planted a bug on her," Cat drawled, watching her friend reach over in the car and kiss his girlie goodbye.

"What do you mean?" asked Anna.

"Well," Cat laughed, "he's in a real state – he thinks I'm going to be a total bitch tonight, and stir it up for him with Gabrielle."

"How do you know he thinks that?" asked Kerry, her eyes glued to the snog-a-thon going on below.

"He phoned me up last night and told me!" Catrina cackled, obviously enjoying Matt's discomfort about leaving his girlfriend alone and defenceless with her. "He told me I'd better not blab about us two having gone out together in front of Gaby."

"But you wouldn't, would you?" asked Anna

hopefully. She certainly didn't want any scenes on her first ever night of 'entertaining'.

"No, of course not!" said Cat, looking slightly hurt, as if dropping Matt in it was something she'd never, ever been guilty of. "Matt's not going to be here tonight, so what would be the point? I do it to wind him up and if I can't have the pleasure of seeing him squirm, then there's no fun in it, is there?"

A movement from below – Gabrielle finally getting out of the car – made all three girls duck out of sight behind the swathe of aqua-blue sari material pinned up at the window.

They couldn't help giggling at the glimpse they'd caught of Matt's panic-stricken face.

• • •

"I'm sorry, Maya, but you're a real disappointment," Cat tutted, leaning back against the sofa, her arms folded across her chest.

"Oh, yes? And why's that?" asked Maya, who'd only recently arrived at the flat above the End, breathlessly hurrying from her photography club.

"You go all the way to Florence and don't even snog any beautiful Italian boys. Not one!" Cat exclaimed.

"I told you, Cat – I wasn't on a Club 18-30 holiday! This was just a sightseeing, *family* holiday. *You* try flirting when you've got two parents and an obnoxious sister hovering about, never mind having a seven-year-old welded to your hand!"

Cat stretched over to the basket of tortilla chips Gabrielle was passing round and grabbed a handful.

"Thanks, Gabs. Well, I have to say, Maya, if it was *me*, I'd have managed *some*how..."

"I bet you would," replied Maya, flicking through the Polaroids Cat had passed to her the moment she got in. "These look good, Cat!"

The Polaroids were of the make-up designs Cat had come up with at Winstead CFE for the upcoming Christmas show. Kerry, Gabrielle and Anna had already seen and admired them.

"Listen, Maya – I've got a favour to ask," said Cat, abandoning her teasing for a second. "We'll need some photos done soon for the posters to advertise the show. Would you be up for doing them?"

"Yes! Of course!" Maya grinned. "I'd love to!"

"At least it would make up for not doing Sonja's shoot..." said Kerry quietly. She guessed that Maya would have probably been hurt that her role had been so easily replaced by Billy, reading between the lines of what Sonja had told her about their original conversation.

"That's a point, where is my super-dooper-model cousin?" asked Cat. "Don't tell me the contract from Tommy Hilfiger has come through already!"

"Cat! Don't be so horrible!" Kerry reprimanded her, but couldn't help giggling. "She said she was coming; I don't know what could have happened to her..."

Anna hadn't said anything yet, but she'd been getting edgy about Sonja's no-show – first, because she thought Sonja might still be bearing some kind of grudge about their disagreement, and second, because everyone was starting to get hungry. The Mexican food Anna had been preparing for tonight was just ready to heat up, once all the guests had finally arrived.

"Well, I say stuff her. I'm starving and whatever you've got in that pot over there...?"

"Refried beans," Anna answered Cat's question.

"Mmm, refried beans – get it on, Anna! Sonja can have hers cold, if she ever turns up!"

Anna shot a jokey salute in Cat's direction and happily went over to the kitchen area of her small living room/diner. The set-up wasn't exactly luxurious, but at least it meant that, being only a few feet away, she could still join in the conversation while she cooked.

Or hear the doorbell.

"Sonja, hi! Come in!" Anna ushered her inside.

"Sorry I'm late, Anna," said Sonja, breezing in. "Hi, everyone. Sorry, got held up. I've been having a few hassles with my mother."

Sonja pulled off her coat, threw it on a chair without making any comment about Anna's flat and flopped herself on the sofa next to Kerry.

"What hassles?" asked Kerry, who almost felt one of the Harvey family, she'd known them so long. "You *never* have hassles with your mum!"

"Well, I do now!" Sonja said, running her fingers through her honey-blonde hair. "She went ballistic at me for going to see that modelling agency on Monday!"

"Doesn't she want you to model?" asked Gabrielle, who only knew the bare bones of the modelling saga. Matt's lack of interest in the subject had meant she was spared from the mind-numbing coverage the others had had to listen to.

"Mmm, well, she's not too happy, but after a bit of a row last night, I finally managed to persuade her tonight to let me go ahead with it," Sonja answered, without actually looking at Gabrielle.

Although Sonja had felt terrible when Matt stormed out the night before, she'd managed to forget it pretty quickly in light of her own troubles. That was, until Gabrielle's presence had reminded her just now. There was no edginess about Gabrielle, Sonja noticed, so Matt obviously hadn't told her about their falling-out.

"So Billy's pictures worked out well then?" asked Maya magnanimously.

"Kind of," shrugged Sonja. "I mean, they got me an appointment, but my agent – Tony – says they're not really good enough. I'm getting more shots done this weekend, actually, in a professional studio."

"This weekend? Wow, they're not wasting much time!" said Kerry, trying hard to sound intrigued. She could sense that Maya was offended for Billy's sake and that Cat was an inch away from saying something sarky. By jumping in first, she might avert a bad atmosphere, she reckoned.

"I know," nodded Sonja. "And that's why I needed to talk Mum round. I need money to pay for this photo shoot *and* for my agency joining fee, of course."

Anna, standing back at the cooker, was about to question what Sonja had just said: from everything she'd read, proper agencies *never* made you pay for anything like that. But after getting her tongue bitten off once already when she'd offered an opinion, Anna chose to stay silent and carried on with her stirring.

Only Maya was brave enough to tackle it.

"Son – I hate to say this, but it doesn't sound quite right; you having to shell out like that. Shouldn't you talk to someone like Natasha to see if this agency's playing straight with you?"

Out of the corner of her eye, Anna saw a shadow cross Sonja's face and expected the worst. But before Sonja could speak, Kerry let out a groan.

"Ooh, don't say that name! You make me feel so guilty!"

"How come, Kez?" asked Cat.

"I spoke to Ollie earlier," Kerry grimaced, "and he seemed to be hinting so strongly that I should bring Tasha along here tonight, since she's at home all by herself!"

"Well, why didn't you ask her? What's she like? Isn't she nice?" asked Gabrielle, again not quite up to speed with everyone's histories.

At Gabrielle's question, Cat gave an involuntary snort of derision.

Anna was instantly aware of tensions rising and felt herself watching like an observer from her spot by the cooker. Kerry, she knew, didn't particularly like Natasha – partly because they had nothing in common and Natasha never made the effort, and partly because of the strain Natasha had put on Kerry's own friendship with Sonja at the start of the summer. When Kerry had come out with that little outburst just now, she must've forgotten that Sonja was sitting right beside her and that Sonja still – despite the fact that Natasha had been offhand the last time they'd met – considered her a friend.

The other problem with mentioning Natasha was, of course, that she'd gone out with Matt, and that thorny subject was one that had to be avoided with Gabrielle in the room.

Could Cat stick to her promise and keep her mouth shut? Surprisingly, she could – only someone else couldn't.

"There's nothing wrong with Tasha," said Sonja, turning to Gabrielle. "Catrina just doesn't like her because she nicked Matt off her."

Only the simmering bubble of refried beans broke the silence in the room.

CHAPTER 18

● ●

MATT MISSES THE POINT

"I can't *believe* Sonja said that!" Cat shook her head, then licked the cappuccino froth off her spoon.

"I can't believe she got in and goofed before *you*," Maya answered.

"I can't believe Gabrielle swallowed that cover-up you guys tried!" said Anna, joining the other two girls during her break for a post-mortem of the night before.

"I know, but what else could we do?" said Maya. "Mind you, once I'd explained it was a totally *different* Matt Sonja had meant, it might have worked better if Kerry hadn't kept gabbling, 'It's not *your* Matt, Gabrielle! Sonja didn't mean *him*!' over and over again."

"Still, I think we managed to cover it up OK,"

Cat said with certainty. Even though she didn't feel certain at all.

Maya and Anna nodded their agreement. Even though they were both even less certain than Cat.

• • •

"Happy?"

"Oh, yes," smiled Gabrielle, although Matt couldn't see her face. He was lying behind her on the huge leather sofa, his arms wrapped around her as they watched some old episodes of *Friends* on video.

"Good," said Matt, giving her a little squeeze.

"Don't know if my parents would be..." she laughed.

"Would be what?" asked Matt, feeling so lazily content that he wasn't concentrating too hard.

"Happy... Happy if they knew that I come and hang out at an eighteen-year-old boy's house so often and that his dad's usually never here!"

Matt released his hold on her and pushed himself up on one elbow to see her better.

"Then why don't I meet them some time? Just so they know you're going out with someone who cares about you? I mean, you know my dad, right?"

"Matt, I've met your dad twice and both times,

all we've said is 'hello', 'cause he's been on his way out somewhere," she smiled. "I wouldn't say I actually *know* him!"

"Yeah, OK, but what about it?" Matt said earnestly. "Go on – why don't I meet your parents some time? Wouldn't that be a good idea?"

Even as the words were leaving his lips, Matt could imagine his friends' reaction if they'd heard what he'd just come out with. Matt volunteering to meet a girlfriend's parents. In the past, he'd have run a mile if a girl had suggested it. Meeting parents ranked right up there with visits to dentists, getting a 'proper' job or smashing his precious music collection with a mallet, as far as Matt was concerned.

At least it had in the old days. Before he fell for Gabrielle.

"Mmm... maybe," shrugged Gabrielle, a fleeting frown crossing her brow.

Matt gazed down at her perfect face, her soft brown skin, her huge dark Bambi eyes and wondered what she wasn't telling him.

"You have told them about me, haven't you?" he suddenly realised.

"No, I haven't," she answered simply.

"Well, why not?" asked Matt, the hurt apparent in his voice.

"You could also ask – why?"

"Huh?"

"Why? Why should I tell them who I'm going out with?"

"Because... because we love each other!" Matt reasoned.

"Yeah!" Gabrielle giggled in his arms. "But we're not exactly getting married or anything, Matt!"

Matt felt stupidly let down. She was right in some ways, but he felt hurt that he didn't seem worthy of taking home and being introduced to her family.

"But I thought they knew you were going out with someone..." he almost whimpered.

"Well, they know I've been out on a few dates with someone, yes; but they haven't asked for more details and I haven't offered any!"

"But your sister knows about me because she was there when we met..."

"Yes, and she tells me about the boys she's seeing. But we just talk about it together; we don't sit and discuss it with Mum and Dad! Do you?"

Matt said nothing, but looked off towards the widescreen TV where *Friends* was still playing, unwatched.

"What's up?" asked Gabrielle, lifting her hand to his dark hair and rubbing her long, cool fingers through it.

"It's just..." Matt struggled to put his disappointment into words. "It's just that I think it's a bit weird, keeping me a secret like that."

"We all have our little secrets, Matt," she smiled knowingly at him, but he seemed lost in his own thoughts, staring blankly at the TV.

On-screen, Rachel, Monica and Phoebe were all lying around on sofas gossiping, which brought Matt's mind back round to the girls' night at Anna's.

"So you enjoyed yourself last night then?" he asked, changing the subject and hoping this foolish feeling of hurt pride would leave him.

"Matt, that's only about the fifth time you've asked me!"

"I know, but I just wanted to check the girls had been nice to you..."

He knew he was sounding pathetic – just like Ross on *Friends* – but he couldn't help it. He'd spent the whole of the previous evening biting his nails with worry over what Cat might be saying to his darling girl. He didn't trust Cat one iota, even though she'd promised him over the phone that she wouldn't go meddling.

"Like I told you already, they were all lovely to me, Matt. In fact we had some really interesting conversations..."

But Matt missed what she was saying as the

mobile phone he'd left on the table warbled loudly into life.

"Sorry, sorry – I better get this in case it's a job," he apologised, stretching over her to grab it. "Hello? Yeah, Billy? Hi – what's up? God, I forgot all about that. Right, OK, thanks. Talk to you later."

Gabrielle gazed up into his face as a frown crossed his brow.

"Anything wrong?" she asked him, aware that a perfect moment to get him to talk might have just slipped by.

"Nothing drastic, but pretty urgent. I was meant to pick up an amp for The Loud's gig earlier. I'd better phone Ollie and see if he can rearrange a time with the guy he's borrowing it from," he explained, punching in the number of the flat above The Swan.

Gabrielle sighed, now *sure* that the moment had well and truly gone.

"Ollie!" barked Matt down the line, before stuttering awkwardly, "Oh, it– it's you..."

Gabrielle watched as his face, just above her, turned pink. With the phone so close, she could make out the faraway female voice that was answering back.

"Uh... yeah, yeah, it's Matt. Oh... he's not there? If you could just tell—? Yes, thanks. Er, bye."

"All right?" asked Gabrielle, perfectly aware that he'd got through to Natasha.

Natasha, who – as she'd found out the night before – he'd once dated.

"Yeah, I, er, it was his mum," Matt lied pathetically.

CHAPTER 19

• •

ALL THAT GLITTERS...

"Right, let's go!" boomed Tony, closing the door to First Call Models and leading the way up the stairs.

"I've got about five changes of clothes with me, and I've brought some clips and scrunchies and things so I can change my hairstyle too..." Sonja panted as she tried to keep up with him bounding up the steps two at a time.

"Good, good. Great stuff," said Tony, stopping suddenly outside a door on the next landing. He took out a bunch of keys, unlocked the door and motioned her to go inside.

"Destiny Awaits Dating Agency?" Sonja found herself saying, reading the sign on the door.

"Yep, my daughter Hayley runs this part of the business. Straight through – the studio's behind that white door there."

Sonja's heart sank; the modelling agency and this dating agency were all part of the same business? That didn't sound very cutting edge.

"Er... and the company on the top floor?" she asked tentatively.

"Doggy Locks? The grooming parlour? Yes, my wife Pauline runs that," he replied, his chest puffed out with pride. "Keep it all in the family, eh?"

Sonja smiled a watery smile and tried to think herself positive about the forthcoming shoot. She'd almost had to keep this afternoon in the family too – her mother had been determined that she was going to accompany Sonja to the shoot, just to check out what sort of business it was that her daughter was getting involved in.

It had taken a lot of persuasion (and a bit of lying) to talk her out of it. It wouldn't look professional, Sonja had explained, taking your mum along, and had promised faithfully that Maya would be with her.

Maya, however, was with her grandparents this Saturday afternoon, completely unaware that her name had been used in vain.

"The photographer's not here yet then?" asked Sonja, glancing around the small studio, with its well-used equipment.

"What's that?" asked Tony.

"The photographer – he's not here yet?"

"You're looking at him, Sonja, love! Anthony Jones, at your service!" he grinned widely at her. "Didn't you realise I was the photographer?"

"Oh... oh, no I didn't," Sonja stumbled, hoping the disappointment wasn't blindingly obvious from her face.

"Right, it's going to take a bit of time to get the lighting and backdrop set up, Sonja, so why don't you stick the kettle on and make us a cup of tea? Fantastic! And have a look at some of the pictures while you start getting ready," he beamed, pointing at the various photos and magazine pages pinned to the walls. "See the kind of poses we'll be going for today."

Sonja slapped what she hoped would look like an enthusiastic smile on her face and wandered over to a worktop where a kettle and mugs stood.

Come on, Sonja – it's not what you thought it would be like, but it's still the real deal! she tried to convince herself. *You can be out there modelling soon, earning money, doing something glamorous – and showing the others what you're capable of!*

After filling the kettle at a sink in a paint-peeling bathroom, Sonja came back into the studio and was pleased to hear that Tony had put on some music. At least it would create a little atmosphere. Even if Phil Collins wasn't her choice of easy listening.

"Like I say, check out some of the work," he said above the track that was playing. "That's the kind of top-quality jobs you'll be doing soon! Big bucks, Sonja, big bucks!"

Sonja smiled and turned her attention to the walls.

Rows of attractive men and women with identikit toothy smiles beamed back at her.

"That's Erica," said Tony, appearing suddenly at her side. "Been with us about five years now. Never out of work."

Gazing at the young woman – perkily perched on the edge of a settee under the slogan that read *Al comfort at Sammy's Cut-price Sofas!* – Sonja wasn't sure what to say.

It wasn't Gap, that was for sure.

"And this is Sadie," Tony told her, pointing to a girl perched perkily on the bonnet of a car with a bucket and sponge in her hands. "Bubbles Hand Car Wash – I tell you, their business rocketed when this ad hit the local free paper!"

Sonja felt a cold shudder down her back. If anyone from college saw her in a corny ad like that, she'd be laughed out of class.

"And, um, this one?" asked Sonja, feeling that she had to respond somehow.

"Ah that, yes," nodded Tony, looking at the newspaper photo of some girls strolling on a catwalk in what looked suspiciously like nylon pinnies. "Twelve of my models did that show. That was for Worthington's Workwear – y'know, overalls and the like. Look, there – in the background in the butcher's apron – that's Ben. Our top male model."

"Tony, I was wondering..." Sonja interrupted.

"Yes, love?"

"Do you ever get jobs for things like local clothes designers?"

"Local designers? Nah, they don't have the money for it," he shook his head, in a split second dispelling the image Sonja had in her head of being the face of the next fledgling Vivienne Westwood.

"Oh..." she muttered non-committally.

"Y'see, established companies like Worthington's, and our other regulars, like Bernard's – y'know, the big plumbing contractors? They've got the cash and understand the benefit of getting a pretty face to sell their product. And, of course," Tony beamed, sweeping his arm over the cuttings on the wall with fatherly pride, "any of these could be your contract next, Sonja! What do you say to that?"

Sonja knew exactly what to say.

"No thanks," she replied coolly, scooping up her coat and sports bag and heading for the door.

CHAPTER 20

● ●

THE GATECRASHER (PART 2)

The garden was full of vampires, ghosts and witches – plus a stray Batman or two.

None of the kids at Lewis's birthday-cum-Halloween-cum-Guy Fawkes party seemed to mind the biting cold air; they all were too busy bobbing for apples, screaming at the top of their voices and waiting impatiently for their burgers and hot dogs to appear. After that, they were to be taken round to the nearby park to watch the organised fireworks display.

Kerry, who'd grovelled to Mr Hardy and got a half day off her Saturday job at the chemist's specially, had her own tasks to perform. Now that it was getting dark, she walked around the garden and lit in turn each of the nightlights that lay inside the carved pumpkin lanterns dotted around the flower borders. They looked fantastic and all the children gasped with delight at the sight of each illuminated head with its spiky-toothed grin.

Despite being hectically busy in her role as party co-ordinator, Kerry still had time to feel a little disgruntled that none of her friends had come along to join in the silliness and wish Lewis a happy birthday.

Ollie had good reason – The Loud's gig was happening later that night and he, Joe and Matt (as general helper-outer) were all at the venue, soundchecking and setting up. Maya, along with Ravi, had been all set to come, until their grandparents had decided to arrive for a weekend visit.

Apart from that, Anna was working, Cat had bottled out ("Lewis is cute, Kerry, but a whole pack of noisy kids? No thanks!") and Sonja? Well, Sonja had better things to do. Like travel to the city and pose around a photographer's studio.

("You *will* make it back for the gig, though, won't you, Son?" Ollie had asked her. "Well, I'll just have to see how things go," she'd shrugged in reply.)

"KERRYKERRYKERRY!" yelped Lewis, in the shape of a warlock, appearing magically at his sister's side. "Molly's crying because Aaron bit her!"

"I did not bite her! I was only pretending! I'm Count Dracula – see?" shouted a small boy in a black cloak, pulling a set of plastic fangs out of his mouth and presenting them to Kerry as evidence.

"OK, OK," nodded Kerry, not wanting to get too close to the drool-dripping fake teeth. She glanced back into the kitchen to where her mum and dad and the couple of sets of parents who'd been brave enough to hang around were now drinking wine and chatting. It would be nice if they came and gave her a hand.

"Right, where's Molly? Let's talk to her and sort this out."

Lewis took one hand and Aaron took the other, and together they led Kerry over to a small, wailing girl who had her arms thrown around something dark and furry.

"Molly?" asked Kerry.

The girl released her stranglehold on Barney long enough for him wriggle free and bound off towards the sausage rolls on the picnic table. Her howls at his desertion were louder than her sobs at having been 'got' by Dracula.

Between trying to pacify Molly and to calm the indignant Aaron who was still insisting that he'd only *pretended* to bite Molly, Kerry didn't hear her mother calling her at first.

"Kerry! *Kerry!*" she shouted more insistently

from the kitchen doorway at her daughter. "Someone here for you!"

Extricating herself from the Dracula drama, Kerry walked back into the house, wondering who it could be. At first she wondered if Sonja or Maya had been able to make it after all, but she knew it couldn't be them – her mother would have just sent them straight through to the garden.

"Hi," said the girl standing awkwardly in the kitchen, a gift-wrapped parcel in her hands.

Kerry had never seen Natasha look awkward and it took her by surprise, apart from the shock of her just turning up at all.

"Ollie said I should come along – with this..." she held up the parcel "...since he couldn't make it himself."

Well, thought Kerry, *I don't believe it!*

• • •

The two girls, along with hundreds of other spectators in Winstead park, craned their necks as they watched the display above them.

"This reminds me of being a kid!"

Kerry stole a look at Natasha and marvelled at the natural, happy expression on her face. The spangles of light from the fireworks showered pinks, blues, yellows and greens across her perfect features, which tonight seemed more like that of a child than a model.

"Mmm, this lot are having fun, that's for sure," Kerry agreed, looking at the huddle of giggling, shrieking children in front of them.

In the middle of the huddle was the birthday boy, waving his greeny-luminous rubber toy skeleton around – Ollie's gift via Natasha.

Earlier, Natasha had surprised Kerry (yet again) by joining in the kids' games with good spirit after she'd arrived, even if she had been a little self-conscious at first. Molly had attached herself to the "pretty lady" like a limpet and had only let go of Natasha when it seemed as if the other kids would beat her in the scramble to get coats on to go to the park.

"I haven't had this much fun in ages!" Natasha positively beamed.

Kerry stared at Ollie's twin in surprise: since she was sixteen, this girl had lived in a flat in one of London's trendiest areas, jetting off to countries Kerry had only ever seen in magazines and with access to star-spangled events that only the beautiful and the famous could ever hope to attend. How could a kiddy party in a drab little town compare?

Instead of saying all that, the only thing Kerry came out with was, "How come?"

Natasha turned to face Kerry with eyes wide and direct.

"This is all just straightforward, silly, honest fun. It's *real*, isn't it?"

Kerry wasn't sure what she meant and even in the dark, her expression must have said as much.

"Well, London, my job... I thought both of them would be brilliant, y'know? But it's so fake."

Kerry nodded vaguely, still not clear what Tasha was getting at. A brilliant career, success, independence... It sounded pretty amazing compared to being at sixth-form college, living with your parents in sleepy old Winstead.

"Lately... I've just kind of had enough," said Natasha wistfully.

"Why's that?" Kerry gently pushed her.

"Well, lots of things. You know that last magazine shoot I was in?"

Kerry hadn't seen the fabled blink-and-you'll-miss-the-clothes session, but she'd heard enough about it from Ollie, Sonja and the others.

"Yeah, what about it?" she said, pulling her browny-red curls back from her face and bundling them into the band that she had round her wrist.

"The photographer who took those pictures – his name's Jack, he's twenty-seven and he's kind of *it* at the moment on the magazine scene. And, um, well, we went out for a while."

"Oh," said Kerry, wondering if they'd gone out *before* the revealing fashion shoot (had he used his influence as her boyfriend to get her to do it?) or after (had he seen so much of her that he wanted to see more?).

Natasha answered the question without Kerry asking it.

"He asked me out after the shoot and that was two months ago. Then I found out a couple of weeks ago that he makes a hobby of dating all the youngest, newest models on all the agencies' books, *and* that he'd started seeing someone behind my back."

That sounded horrible to Kerry – heartless, cold and deeply insensitive. No wonder Natasha had come home to lick her wounds.

"But one bad guy shouldn't put you off your job and everything," she tried to reason.

"Yes, but you know how I share a flat?"

Kerry nodded, remembering what Ollie had told her; their parents' condition for Natasha moving to London so young was that she was supposed to be in a 'supervised' flat, looked after by one of the bookers from the agency, along with other young models who'd been signed up.

"The girl I've been sharing a room with – Emily – it turned out *she* was the one Jack was seeing behind my back. And when I confronted her, she told me he'd promised to get her on the cover of one of the big European glossy mags. And she thought I should understand that!"

Kerry shuddered; it sounded so horribly seedy.

"But surely not everyone's like that?" she asked Natasha.

"Maybe not," the other girl shrugged, "but so many people I've got to know in this business are ruthlessly ambitious or self-obsessed or bitchy. I don't know if I can take it any more! Not to mention the whole cattle market of being paraded around different casting directors: having them look you up and down like a piece of meat and then reject you."

Kerry was temporarily lost for words. She'd always suspected that modelling wasn't as glamorous as it sounded, but Natasha was most definitely not painting a very pretty picture.

"Was that why you weren't saying much when Sonja was asking you about it?" Kerry pointed out.

"Yeah, well, I just couldn't be a hypocrite and tell her it's fantastic when I don't feel like that at the moment."

"Never mind," Kerry tried to sound constructive. "At least you're giving yourself a bit of a breathing space at home."

"But that's the thing, Kerry," said Natasha

earnestly. "Nowhere feels like home now. London isn't where I feel comfy and settled and then, when I come back here, my old friends treat me like some snob and don't want to hang about with me any more."

Kerry thought of the gang of girls Natasha had gone around with at school – all pretty, all confident, and all bitches obviously, since they'd dumped their mate when she'd had a sniff of success. Kerry had always assumed it was the other way round, but maybe she'd been wrong.

She was suddenly acutely aware of how lonely Natasha must be, no matter how successful or popular she appeared.

"Listen, Tasha – will you help me get ready to go out to Ollie's gig tonight? I haven't a clue what to wear," she smiled.

"Yes! Yes, I'd love to!" Natasha giggled, then gasped as a firework burst into a huge silvery umbrella of light above their heads.

CHAPTER 21

· ·

COMING BACK DOWN TO EARTH

Anna stood back from the mirror and turned this way and that.

She had never managed to get her hair to sit as gorgeously as it had when Cat had given her a make-over, but – parted in the middle and hanging long and shiny and straight – it still looked pretty good.

Glancing at a clock on her chest of drawers, Anna realised she'd have to get a move on. The Loud were due on stage in forty minutes and she wanted to get down to The Bell and find the others in plenty of time before the gig started.

A functional grin to the mirror revealed no tell-tale signs of spinach in her teeth from her hastily heated up and eaten cannelloni.

"Well, you'll never be picked to be the next

face of Revlon or whatever," she laughed at her reflection. "But tonight, Anna Michaels, you don't look too bad at all!"

Grabbing a tiny tub from the bathroom shelf, Anna was just about to apply some glossy lip balm when the doorbell made her jump.

• • •

"Boo!"

Matt, who'd been standing alone at the bar, turned to see Cat grinning by his side, her hair bundled up into messy bunches, her ample chest vying for prominence with the giant sequinned star sewn to the front of her bright orange T-shirt.

"Hi, Cat," he nodded at her, glad of the company. He'd left the boys back stage getting vibed up for their performance, and had been scanning the crowd for the last ten minutes for any sightings of his friends.

"No Siamese twin tonight then?" Cat asked with a wicked smile.

"What?"

"No Gabrielle? You two *are* normally joined at the hip, aren't you?"

"Oh, right," said Matt, just getting her dig. "No, well, yes. I mean, she should be here soon. She's bringing her mates along."

"Mmm. Any of the rest of our lot here?"

"Nah, not much of a turnout so far. Anna's definitely coming. Maya can't make it — she phoned Ollie to say her grandparents are here for a visit."

Cat made a yawning action.

"OK, that's Maya's excuse," she drawled. "But where's Kerry? I thought she'd be right down at the front of the stage being Ollie's one-woman fan club."

"She should be here, but she had her little brother's party on, remember?"

"God, yes!" Cat pulled a face in horror. "It'll take ages to wash all that ice cream and cake and kiddy sick off her!"

"It's seven-year-olds we're talking about, Cat, not babies!"

"Same difference," shrugged Cat. "And what about Sonja, or should I say Mighty Miss Blabbermouth?"

"She's got that photo shoot on. But why do you call her that?"

"Oh, only that she totally spilled the beans to Gabrielle the other night at Anna's. About you and me, I mean. And you and Natasha," Cat smirked, enjoying the double-whammy of getting her cousin into trouble and relishing the sight of Matt's pained expression.

"What?" he winced.

"Don't worry – Maya managed to cover it up, so Gabrielle didn't suss," she said casually. "Well, at least, I don't *think* she did..."

Matt hid his face in his hands and let out a long, low groan.

"Stop it with the cow impersonations," Cat chided him, before adding brightly, "Here's comes your girlfriend!"

• • •

For a split second when she pulled open the door, Anna couldn't make out who was standing in front of her: the girl's head was bowed and the yellowy glare of the bulb that illuminated the top of the metal stairwell cast a bleached-out cloak of light over the figure clutching a sports bag.

"Can I come in?" said the girl, raising her head at last.

"'Course you can," Anna replied, her intuition telling her that Sonja had something on her mind.

• • •

Ollie and the boys were waiting impatiently for the next fifteen minutes to pass so they could get it over with and step out on stage. Their tension was all the worse because Nick – who'd promised faithfully to tell them who the important person would be in their audience before they took to the stage – was nowhere to be seen.

"Maybe it's better if we *don't* know," said Andy, busy tuning his guitar.

"Yeah, Andy's right. Maybe if we *did* know it was definitely some record company guy to see us, we'd get too nervous and go to pieces."

Joe, who was struck dumb with nerves, looked across silently at Ollie and waited to see what he thought.

"But not knowing who's out there is going to make us just as nervous!" said Ollie, kicking the leg of his chair irritably. He pulled up the bottom of his baggy khaki T-shirt and wiped the beads of sweat off his forehead with it.

"Hey, guys!" said a voice as a jokey punch landed on Ollie's exposed belly. "Miss me?"

"Oufff!" gasped Ollie, though the 'blow' had hardly touched him.

He yanked his T-shirt away from his face and found himself staring at his grinning uncle and another bloke, dressed as a Nick-a-like in jeans, rock T-shirt and leather jacket. He looked slightly familiar, but Ollie couldn't think why.

"Where've you *been*, Nick? We're on soon and we thought our manager would've been here to wish us well!"

"And here I am!" he beamed, holding his arms out wide.

"I *could* say you're cutting it a bit fine and have a rant at you, but what about you just put us out of our misery and let us know what's going on?" Ollie said pointedly.

"Of course, of course. Lads, I'd like you to meet Derek, the guy you've got to impress tonight."

Ollie and the boys nodded at the Nick-a-like, who nodded back at them.

Derek... thought Ollie. *I recognise that guy. Just can't remember where from...*

"Lads, if Derek likes what he hears tonight – and I keep telling him he will – he could have a very sweet offer for you!"

"Oh, yeah?" said Billy, his eyes (like Joe's and Andy's) were wide with excitement. "What's that then?"

"I'm looking for a band to do a regular spot at my gaff," said Derek. "Playing every Thursday night."

"That sounds good," said Billy, with slightly less enthusiasm. Obviously, Derek *wasn't* some flashy A&R man from a London record company, about to waft a big, fat contract under their noses. But then, they'd never really expected that he would be.

Ollie, who'd been staring at Derek, suddenly sat bolt upright.

"Wait a minute! You're the bloke that runs the Railway Tavern!"

"Yes, that's right," Derek nodded and smiled, apparently chuffed to be recognised. He was totally unaware of the shoulders sagging around him as the members of The Loud realised that it wasn't a record deal they were playing for; just a residency at the pub in the station along from the End-of-the-Line café.

"Hey, lads, it'll be great experience for you!" Nick tried to jolly them along. "And, of course, if you manage to pull in enough punters, Derek's willing to pay you £50 a night!"

Ollie, Joe, Andy and Billy exchanged glances at the mention of money and slowly the grins returned to their faces.

"I think we can do business, Derek," beamed Ollie, stretching over to shake the pub landlord's hand.

• • •

"Oh, Anna, I'm *so* embarrassed – I've made such a fool of myself!"

"No, you haven't, Sonja," Anna tried to soothe her, pushing a mug of tea into her hands. "You tried something and it didn't work out – that's all."

"But I've been boasting on and on about it to

all the others. How can I turn round now and say it's not going to happen; that the agency was so Mickey Mouse that it shared premises with a doggy hairdresser?"

"Could be worse..." said Anna, with a little smile on her face.

"How?" Sonja whined.

"They could have asked you to be in an ad for the doggy hairdresser!"

Sonja managed an involuntary snigger. "Mmm, think how proud my friends would be if they saw me, pointing and grinning at some puffed-up poodle!"

Anna was pleased to see that Sonja could laugh at the situation. Her ego had taken a real bashing, so it showed that she had a good spirit to be able to see the funny side.

Then Sonja's smile faded and a sadness came across her eyes.

Anna didn't need intuition to tell her that something else was also troubling her friend.

● ● ●

"Cat looks like she's made some new friends!" said Gabrielle, speaking directly into Matt's ear, so she could be heard above the music blasting from the stage.

"Definitely!" agreed Matt, bending down slightly to talk to his girlfriend. "She told me earlier that they're a couple of Dutch guys who've been hanging around at the End. She's found out that they're taking a break from a round-the-world trip to stop here for a couple of months with relatives, and brush up on their English. So two for the price of one – that should keep her pretty busy!"

"Well, speaking of romance," continued Gabrielle, standing on tiptoe, "Jasmine says she fancies Andy!"

Matt looked over at the band and saw how Jasmine might be attracted to Andy; with his black, spiky hair and the groovy way he moved as he played, it was no surprise that Gabrielle's mates, along with quite a few other girls, were clustered round his side of the stage.

"Didn't she say she fancied Joe when she came to my party?" asked Matt.

"Yes, but she says Andy looks cooler."

"Well, I think Jasmine should go back to fancying Joe," Matt laughed.

"How come?" asked Gabrielle.

"Didn't I tell you? Andy's gay!"

"Is he?" gasped Gabrielle, her eyes wide with surprise. "What a waste..."

"I don't suppose he sees it that way," grinned

Matt. "Listen, Gaby, do you want to come with me to the bar?"

Matt's heart was pounding – he wanted to get Gabrielle over to the back of the room where he might be heard a little better. In the light of what had happened at Anna's, Matt knew he had to get everything off his chest.

"What's up?" asked Gabrielle, once they'd pushed their way through the crowd – a crowd that included Natasha and Kerry, looking very matey all of a sudden.

Matt took a deep breath and let it all out.

"Gaby, when you first asked me about past girlfriends, I didn't exactly tell you the whole truth. I didn't just go out with a couple of girls. I've been out with—"

"Natasha and Cat?" Gabrielle finished the sentence for him, looking him straight in the eye.

Matt stared stupidly at her.

"How did you...? The other night at Anna's; I thought you hadn't..."

"Sussed what Sonja was saying?" Gabrielle suggested, again helping him out with his vanishing words. "Yeah, I did; it was pretty obvious, even though Maya tried to cover it up."

"I, uh..." Matt mumbled uselessly.

"Why didn't you tell me before?" she asked, looking at him with her huge brown eyes. Her expression didn't seem accusing, but Matt felt himself wilt with the guilt.

"I just didn't want you to get the wrong impression of me," he said lamely.

"But, Matt, why do you think I'd have been bothered about you having a few girlfriends before me?" she gazed up at him, wide-eyed.

'Cause it was more than just a few... he thought, but just shrugged apologetically instead.

"So, did you ask Cat and your friends to keep it quiet from me, that you'd gone out together?"

"Yes," nodded Matt, staring at his feet.

"How come?"

"Well, Cat's just a bit..." Matt struggled to find a tactful word to describe her. He couldn't, so he just let the sentence peter out.

A soft, cool hand reached up and stroked his cheek.

"You're such an idiot, aren't you, Matt?" said Gabrielle. "I love you and you love me – that's all that matters."

He looked at her smiling face and felt his heart flip over.

"Are all fourteen-year-old girls as wise as you?" he smiled back at her.

"Are all eighteen-year-old boys as stupid as you?" she grinned back.

Gaby knowing about Cat and Tasha is a real

weight off my mind, Matt thought to himself as he hugged her close. *I'll tell her about the others... later.*

• • •

"It's Owen," said Sonja shyly, aware how sensitive it was to talk to Anna about her own brother.

"What about him?" asked Anna. Last time he'd visited her, she'd hardly seen him after he'd dropped their mother off at the station. He'd spent the rest of the time with Sonja. The two of them seemed to get on so well together, sharing the same lust for life and the same easygoing, happy-go-lucky attitude too.

"I just feel so... so disposable, I guess."

"Disposable? Like 'used'?" Anna raised her eyebrows.

"Oh, no, not like that. He hasn't taken advantage of me or anything," Sonja shook her head. "It's just that me and Owen got on so brilliantly last time he was here and I felt so close to him. And then wham-bam; it's 'see you some time!' He's off on the train with a quick kiss and I never hear from him. Like I was just some casual flirtation while he was here visiting you..."

Anna realised straightaway that this explained

a lot of Sonja's attitude lately. It was as if she was trying to make up for her loss of confidence with Owen by throwing herself into modelling to make herself feel more attractive and wanted again.

But the irony was, she'd got it all wrong about Owen, as Anna knew only too well from the conversations she'd had with him.

"Son, have you ever listened to yourself when you're with Owen?" she began, keen to set Sonja straight.

"What do you mean?"

"You're always wisecracking with him; teasing him about all the girls he must have running after him in Newcastle."

"But I'm only having a laugh!" Sonja protested.

"And that's your problem – you're sending out all these vibes about being independent and see-you-whenever, when what you *really* want is to tell him you're crazy about him and sit talking long-distance mushy stuff down the phone with him every night!"

"But what if he doesn't feel that way about me?"

"Sonja, I'm his sister – trust me, I know. The only reason Owen's been casual about this relationship is because he thinks that's the way *you* want it."

"Really?" squeaked Sonja in surprise.

"*Really*," said Anna firmly. "And right now, I'm going to go and finish putting on my make-up so we can catch at least the end of The Loud's show, while you..."

Sonja took the phone and the address book Anna was shoving into her hands.

"...are going to call a certain someone in Newcastle. OK?"

"OK!" grinned Sonja.

Smiling to herself as she walked towards the bathroom, Anna felt assured that her powers of intuition were right. Sonja and Owen were made for each other, she just knew it.

Sugar
SECRETS...
...& Dramas

SNEAK PREVIEW!

Cat walked into the classroom at the college which was doubling up as the combined make-up and costume area for the Drama Department's Christmas production of Cinderella, and began setting out her overloaded box of cosmetics. As usual, she was the first one there.

As chief make-up artist for the cast, over the last few weeks she'd been practising on various members, including Cinderella and the Ugly Sisters. Not having had too much experience of theatrical make-up so far on her beauty therapy course, Cat was keen to do a good job and was happy putting in the extra hours after college if it meant she'd get the actors' individual looks perfect on the night.

Apart from that, being around actors was what Cat wanted to experience: according to her skewed logic, getting into telly and film work through being a make-up artist was a short-cut to getting into acting. Make contacts, get known – and all without the bother of having to study stuff like Shakespeare and Chekhov for years. Or so Cat reckoned.

For someone who was desperate to act, being involved back stage with the pantomime was also a chance for Cat to soak up the atmosphere. She usually hung around after her stint was over, listening to the cast read through their lines, wishing *she* was Cinderella and not Fran Stevens, who in Cat's opinion had to be the most inappropriate Cinders she'd ever laid eyes on.

(Since when was Cinderella a six-footer? Cat thought cruelly as she eyed up the gangly Fran one day. *She's going to have to bend her knees under her frock or she'll tower over Prince Charming...)*

Cat swung round as she heard the door open. She was expecting it to be Fran, so was surprised when she saw that it was Jeff Patterson, the college's Head of English and Drama, and director of the panto. He had a pile of scripts under one arm, his mobile phone and overstuffed briefcase in the other, and a stressed look on his face.

"Hi, Jeff," Cat smiled. "You're early. I didn't expect you for another half an hour."

He gave her a tense smile in return.

"Got a lot on my mind, Catrina," he said gruffly. "I needed to get here early to try and sort this damn mess out."

Hauling his briefcase on to a table top, he dumped the huge wodge of scripts down beside it and began rifling through the case.

"Anything I can help with?" offered Cat. "I'm working on Fran today, but she hasn't turned up yet so I'm all yours."

"You'll have a long wait," he sighed, running his hand agitatedly through his shock of grey-flecked hair. "She's the reason we're in a mess. She phoned earlier; she's got glandular fever. She's out of the show."

"You're kidding!" Cat gasped, although she knew from his face that he most definitely was not joking. "Well, that's tough luck for Fran, but what's the problem? Abigail Whatsername can take over. She's her understudy..."

"*Was* her understudy. She chucked the course in a couple of days ago and went back home to Scotland. And call me reckless," he added with an ironic smile, "but I didn't think there was the need to have an under-understudy."

"So what will you do?" asked Cat, a glint creeping into her eyes.

"Haven't a clue. Getting someone else to learn her lines and songs in this short a time is going to take a miracle."

Cat gazed at the lecturer as he took off his thick-rimmed glasses and began rubbing his eyes with one hand. She'd come to know him reasonably well over the last few weeks. He was approachable, practical and – at this moment – desperate.

Do it, she told herself sternly.

Without any warning, Cat threw her arms out

and began belting out a song from the show at the top of her voice.

Two minutes later, Jeff was still blinking at her in astonishment through spec-free eyes.

"What was that?" he asked, once his slack-jawed mouth had moved back into action.

"*Some Day My Prince Will Come.* Don't say you didn't recognise it!" said Cat slightly huffily. Her singing voice (though only normally let loose in the shower) wasn't all *that* bad, she was sure.

"Yes, I know what the song was, Catrina," he said, still looking at her quizzically. "Maybe what I should have said was 'why?'"

"Isn't it obvious?"

"Erm, no, I'm afraid it isn't," Jeff shook his head.

"What about *me*?"

Jeff slipped his glasses back on and narrowed his eyes, taking in the vision that was Cat: bleached blonde hair with streaks on either side of her face that seemed the exact same shade as her burgundy lipstick, a crimson, satiny T-shirt that strained alarmingly across her double D-cup chest and a black suede mini that showed an acre of thigh until her legs met her knee-high platform boots.

"What *about* you, Catrina?" the lecturer asked, raising an eyebrow.

"Let me try for the part," Cat gabbled, finding herself grabbing on to the arm of his grey wool jacket. "Go on, *pleeeeeeeease*!!"

"But Catrina – you're not even on the drama course!" protested Jeff.

"Yeah, maybe," shrugged Cat, determined not to be put off. "But I *do* know all of Cinderella's lines; I've been listening to Fran practise them for weeks. I've even helped her go through them!"

"Cat," he said gently, "while I admire your confidence, you have to understand that there's no way I could put you up there on stage in front of a couple of hundred people when you've had no acting experience before in your life. Surely you can see that?"

"Actually, no. I can't," Cat said defiantly. "What I *can* see though is a production that's going to fail – with a capital F – if you don't do something drastic. And that something is me."

Good speech, she praised herself, then saw from Jeff's expression that he still wasn't convinced. She had to think fast.

"Anyway, you don't know *everything* about me. I *have* had acting experience; I was involved in several plays at school."

"Really?" nodded Jeff slowly.

"Really," Cat nodded back. OK, so there hadn't been several plays – only one, and the school happened to be primary. But she had made a brilliant angel in her reception class's production of the Nativity.

Jeff looked from Cat to the pile of stapled pages that lay in front of him, then gave a sigh.

"OK, Catrina – I'll give it a shot," he said, tossing her a script. "Let's have a read-through now."

Cat tried to subdue the grin of triumph that was threatening to break out over her face.

So, I had to tell a little lie to get his attention, she thought. *But isn't acting all about making stuff up?*

ARE YOU A DRAMA QUEEN?

• •

Cat may not be the subtlest person in the world, but when it comes to what she really, really wants, she'll take a risk – even though she might end up looking stupid!

Do you live your life like a soap storyline? Our quiz will help you decide.

I. **What magical thing would you rather have happen to you?**
a) Win £1 million.
b) Be offered Julia Roberts' part in her next Hollywood blockbuster.

2. **In arguments, how do you tend to behave?**
a) Fester, huff, then do the silent thing.
b) Shout, stomp and sometimes blub.

3. **Being in the centre of a room and having all eyes upon you is:**
a) Your worst nightmare come true.
b) Your dream come true.

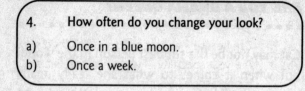

4. How often do you change your look?

a) Once in a blue moon.
b) Once a week.

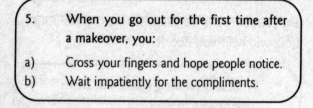

5. When you go out for the first time after a makeover, you:

a) Cross your fingers and hope people notice.
b) Wait impatiently for the compliments.

6. Do you often change the way you talk or act depending on who you're with?

a) No – you try to be the same with everyone.
b) Yes – isn't that what everyone does?

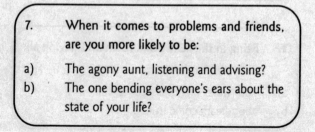

7. When it comes to problems and friends, are you more likely to be:

a) The agony aunt, listening and advising?
b) The one bending everyone's ears about the state of your life?

8.   Surprises...

a)   Can be nice – as long as they're not shocks.
b)   Are your speciality – you get a kick out of
       seeing people's reactions.

9.   When it comes to secrets...

a)   The only ones you really have are the *Sugar
       Secrets* books on the shelf in your bedroom.
b)   You've got one for every day of the week.

10.   Your life is...

a)   Fine, thank you, and you're happiest when
       you feel calm and relaxed.
b)   Like a roller coaster, as your emotions shoot
       up and down and up again – and you love it!

NOW CHECK OUT HOW YOU SCORED...

SO ARE YOU A DRAMA QUEEN?

● ●

An equal mixture of a and b

Looks like you've got the balance right: you know when it's time to be sensible and realistic, but you have your fun moments when you use your natural confidence to shake things up a bit. The difference between you and Cat is that you listen to the sensible voice in your head and never become a fully fledged drama queen, flouncing around and landing yourself in trouble. If life ever seems dull, dump your sensible attitude for a day and take a risk – it might work out better than you ever dreamed!

Mostly a

You know fact from fiction, and you prefer to be realistic and think things through – unlike Cat, who launches herself into everything, good or bad, with 100% energy and no common sense whatsoever. So hurrah for your caution, but remember that taking the odd chance can be quite liberating – and a shedful of fun too! After all, the world would be a much duller place without Cat getting herself into scrapes on a regular basis.

Mostly b

Wow! You're a star-spangled drama queen, whizzing through life like it's going out of fashion. Like Cat, your energy levels and power of imagination are something to be proud of, but your Technicolor slant on the world might not be all that accurate. Keep on bubbling with ideas and enthusiasm, but try pausing for breath instead of plunging headfirst into your next project. Sometimes taking things slowly can make them even better!